Eden Inviolate

About the Author:
The proud son of two 20-year Navy veterans, Don A. Martinez holds a Bachelor of Arts degree in writing, and a Master of Arts degree in English with a focus on myth and folklore, both from Buffalo State College (New York). He works as a college writing professor in Texas, where he lives with his wife, daughter, and four cats.

Other Books by Don A. Martinez:
The Phantom Squadron Series
The Advance Guard
Dinétah Dragon
The Insurgent's Journal
Infernal Eighteen

Eden Inviolate

Don A. Martinez

Desert Coyote Productions

Longview, Texas

Library of Congress Control Number: 2014909374
EAN-13: 978-0-9859379-6-6
ISBN-10: 0985937963

Typeset in 11pt Book Antiqua
Printed in the U.S.A.
First edition 2014

For Stacey, for Kahlan, and for everyone who loves freedom

Contents

"The American monomyth begins and ends in Eden. Stories in this genre typically begin with … townspeople living in harmony. A distruption of harmony occurs, and must be eliminated by the superhero …"
-- **Robert Jewett and John Shelton Lawrence,** ***The American Monomyth***

Excerpt from a Speech before a Joint Session of Congress
by President Carleton Regent
March 22nd, 2031

My fellow Americans, members of Congress, members of the Cabinet, we live in dire, dangerous times. We live in fear, for our lives and for our way of living. We live in constant fear of those who lord over us, who bully us with their words and their actions.

The most simple schoolchild could tell you that this state of affairs is wrong. Morally wrong, spiritually wrong, just plain wrong. The time has therefore come for us to act.

This morning, Vice President Regent passed a document along to me. It sits on my desk in the Oval Office as we speak. This document was prepared by our international intelligence branch of the SSA. I read this report twice, and I still am not quite believing what it contains, but at the same time I have decided that we must act, because our safety is at stake.

This report concerns the activities of our greatest threat to public safety, Alanna Sharpe, the scourge of Chicago. Our sources have confirmed that she is massing an army, training them, organizing them, and preparing for a mass terror attack on a worldwide scale. A supernatural attack, mind you. Her army is made up of nothing but supernaturals like herself, like-minded in their aggression against the peace-loving people of the New Empire and the entire world.

This can not be allowed to stand.

Our sources can only tell us that the army is being massed, but cannot tell us exactly where that massing is taking place. We can't go into this battle blind, as we have done numerous times before when we have placed our citizens in harm's way. We must know what the stakes are. We must know our enemy. We must know their weakness.

If we do not know their location, we at least know the other three qualities. The stakes are the peace and safety of the world, for if any of these supernatural attacks takes place, the bloodshed will be on a genocidal scale. Our enemy is slippery, pernicious, hard to kill, and dedicated to their cause of a supernatural world, with normal people crushed under their boots, or talons, or whatever may be on their feet. Most of all, we know their weakness, and it is their fanatical devotion to the idea that Alanna Sharpe is their savior. Cut off the head, and the snake will perish.

So too will the supernatural threat die once Alanna Sharpe is no more.

Tomorrow I will be presenting our case before the United Nations General Assembly, and attempting to convince those nations who claim to be our allies that our intelligence is correct. Many will doubt us. I daresay that some of them will oppose us vocally. To these nations, I say this: you either stand with us, with the rest of humanity, and fight; or you stand with the supernatural threat, and we will destroy you along with them.

I say this also to anyone within the borders of the New Empire who may still hold any sympathy for the supernatural cause. You will be found, you will be held, and you will know the error of your belief.

To Alanna Sharpe and her confederates, we have this message. We are coming for you. We will find you. Your threat to humankind will not stand, so long as we draw breath. No matter where you are, we will flush you out. There is no place you can go, in this world or any other, where we cannot get to. There is no hope for you.

In light of the information we have received, I therefore request war powers from the Congress, in accordance with the Constitution of the New Empire of America. I request funds to be distributed to the Supernatural Suppression Agency, to be used for international intelligence operations aimed toward finding Alanna Sharpe's supernatural training grounds.

I also request that, should the worst happen and this attack take place, Congress grant permission to declare worldwide war against Alanna Sharpe's supernatural forces. This effort will spread the SSA around the globe, to hunt down and destroy all supernatural activity. I ask this humbly of the body, in the interests of world peace.

God bless us all, and God Bless our New Empire.

Eden Inviolate

Stormfront

Chapter One: Homecoming

July 5th, 2031

I reach up with the remote control in my hand and click off the TV set. I think I've seen enough. My stomach is churning … I think I'm going to be sick.

My level of exhaustion is slightly better than it was yesterday. I hate that I had to spend most of my birthday in bed, because I was too tired to do anything, but what did I expect? I went eighteen days with nothing but water … holy water … to sustain me. I traversed the pits of Hell. I fought demons, I fought ancestors. I found Dad and had a conversation with Lucifer.

Then that even wasn't the biggest shock. My whole world started to crumble on me while I was down in the hole, but when I emerge I find out that things up here got so much worse in my absence, which here was two years. My friends are in hiding, changed, having fought for so long and so hard. My best friend has changed the most … Michika only manhandled me in the morning with her new cat powers, but backed off in the afternoon. Things are so different now.

Yet things stay the same, and that can be comforting. On this early morning, I'm finally snapped out of my stupor in the darkened TV room by the scent of food approaching. I look up and see Aunt Kitty, approaching through the gloom, a plate loaded with food in one hand and a cup of coffee in the other.

No wait, it's not coffee … I can smell it better as she gets closer, it's orange pekoe tea. She sets it down on the table in front of me. "Bad show on the tube?"

I sigh and look up as she sits down next to me. "Yeah. Michi was nice enough to tape this, I guess … so what happened after this speech?" I turn my head slightly as I start eating the meal on the plate, scrambled eggs with two slabs of bison and hash browns.

"Well, as he said, he presented his case before the UN. There was a group of fifteen nations … the media's called them the Super 15 … that mounted the only protest against the plan, and you can probably guess which one led the way."

I nod. "Jordan, right?"

"Got it in one. King Fahai was in attendance at the session, and spoke right after our American Führer. He gave it a go, with an impassioned speech protesting the enlargement of the SSA, claiming … and rightfully so, I might add … that any expansion of anti-supernatural sentiment would be tantamount to the New Empire assuming control of the entire world."

The food tastes good, but it's the situation that's leaving a bitter flavor in my mouth. "Who are the other countries?"

"It doesn't really matter, because none of them have much power in the body, as none of them are currently on the Security Council. Anyway, the night after the session was when King Fahai died, supposedly of a heart attack."

I can imagine what the real cause of death must have been.

"Fahaian left a day later to take his throne."

I nod gravely. "When did Michi change?"

Aunt Kitty rolls her eyes, clearly showing me she doesn't like what she's about to tell me. "A week after Fahaian left. We were in the middle of a fight, because we'd accidentally moved the Ranch into the middle of an SSA compound. One minute she's rushing into the battle, I lose track of her while fighting a bunch of blueshirted bozos, and the next time I see her she's in my old body, wailing away and blasting them with that stupid glove of hers …"

She wipes her eye gently. Something tells me she's very upset about this. "Are you okay, Aunt Kitty?"

She sighs and nods quickly. "I'll be fine. Anyway, once the fight subsided and we were away from the SSA, I had it out with Durga. She had been passing through the night before, wanting to check to see if you had come up from the Inferno yet, and stayed overnight only to get drawn into the battle the next morning. She had no right to make Michi her servant, not when the burden should have been mine. So as a result I kicked her ass permanently out of the Ranch. She's forbidden to ever come back."

This news makes me very sad. Durga has been my favorite teacher, the one who helped me gain control over the Guardswoman, who taught me that control equates to power. Without her to help me, what chance do I have now?

My hand drifts down to the Sword, hanging loosely from my hip. It helped me greatly in Hell, but will the power be enough to confront what's before me now? A worldwide war … I shudder thinking about it.

11

There's more pressing matters, I know, and so I look up at Aunt Kitty, having eaten the final morsel on my plate. "How's Dad doing?"

She lights up slightly. "Better. He's sitting up, eating last I saw him. He's been lying in that bed for two years, so his muscles need some time to adjust to motion again, but his mind's there at least."

I need to see him. I need to be reminded that what I did for eighteen days was real, that I truly did rescue him. Teacup in hand, I leave the TV room and head toward Dad's room.

The door is slightly cracked, with light pouring out, as I approach. I knock gently on the door.

"Come in." The voice isn't Dad's. Unfortunately, it belongs to Gabe Francis. Over the course of this entire period searching for Dad, I've really started hating Gabe's half-truths and convenient misinformation. I'm dreading seeing him now, even though it should be a happy time.

Cheer up, girl. You just saved your dad from hell.

I slowly push the door open, letting the pale light within bathe me. I look over toward the bed and see two upright shadows. One of them turns around to face me, and even in the dimness I can see his white hair and weird eye tattoos.

"Ah, Alanna, I'm glad you're here." Gabe tries to smile. Tries to, because it comes out more as a smirk. It's always a smirk with that man. I'd like to scowl at him, give him a verbal beatdown for the insanity he forced me into in the name of teaching me a lesson, but my fury can't find a voice because of the face close behind him.

Dad's looking up at me, his face hollow and malnourished, but his eyes as clear as they ever were. He smiles over at me. "Hey, little sweetheart."

That melts me. Immediately, I'm at his side, clutching him tightly. He feels so thin …

"Daddy, I'm so glad … so glad you made it." I don't want the waterworks to start right now, not with Gabe in the room. Once he leaves maybe, but not now.

"I'm glad, too." Dad squeezes me gently.

"I hate to interrupt this reunion," Gabe interjects, "but there's some business we need to attend to. Cole was just telling me about you having a talk with Lucifer. I sincerely hope you kept my advice to you in mind."

I turn toward Gabe, but I keep my arm around Dad. "I'm not about to let my guard down around the Devil himself, Gabe."

"What was the talk about?"

I sigh. I don't want to re-live the Inferno ever, but this might be important. "He was asking me for a favor, tried to bargain with me for a task, actually."

Gabe nods, his chin in his hand. "What was it about?"

"Another sword, more powerful than the Sabre of the Invader. It's missing, along with a prince and princess of Hell, and I have a feeling I know where we might find all three."

An eyebrow shoots up on Gabe's face. "What sword? I only knew about the Sabre."

Did I seriously catch Gabe Francis off-guard with new information? Something about this conversation makes me feel powerful. "Lucifer called it the 'Damnation

13

Blade.' It was held in a leather casket, but when it was opened for us the Blade was missing."

Gabe's face goes pale. "Oh God. *That* Blade ... I'd forgotten about it."

Well crap, that didn't last long. "What can you tell us about it? Lucifer didn't say much, other than he offered me a hell of a lot to find it and bring it back."

The agent grumbles under his breath. "Are you sure ..."

"Gabe, please tell her." Dad's voice sounds insistent, and still powerful despite his weakened body.

"All right then," Gabe mutters. "The Damnation Blade, as you might already know, was also forged by Abaddon at the same time as the Sabre of the Invader. The metal was formed from lava collected from the deepest circles of Hell, mingled with Lucifer's own blood. When finished, the Blade was said to be thirteen feet long, larger than any sword anyone save a demon could wield."

This isn't good at all. "I need to know, Gabe. What am I up against? What can the Blade do?"

"Alanna, please ..."

"Tell me!" I'm standing up, nervous. I'm scared out of my mind, the last thing that I need is Gabe holding back on me again.

"Okay. The Damnation Blade can kill gods."

I sink back down to the bed and clutch Dad tightly. *A sword that can kill gods? What good is a Guardsman going to be against something like that?*

"Are you satisfied? The Blade can destroy gods, so you can imagine what it can do to a regular supernatural." Gabe stands up and straightens his tie.

"If you'll excuse me, I need some time to think." He storms out.

I sit down on the bed. I don't think I've ever seen Gabe that rattled in my life. Dad's hand finds mine.

"Are you all right, Alanna?"

"I'm not sure, Dad, it's just … there's just so much stuff down there that I saw … things that I *did* … it's too much for me to process. I'm not sure if I'm going to be any good to anyone up here."

Dad leans forward. It's a great struggle for him to do, but the same hand that was on my own now finds my shoulder. "You can't be expected to carry that burden yourself, not forever. You're going to need to talk through it. God knows I'll need to, I spent so long down there."

For what feels like the first time in an eternity, my eyes meet his. I see the pain, the sadness, the torment that he's been through. All at once, I'm sad for my father but at the same time I'm glad that it's him sitting here and not Tyrelius Scolar. I lean over to him and hug him tightly.

"We'll get through it together, Daddy. I promise."

I think he's weeping … I feel his shoulders shudder. "I missed you so much, Alanna, you and your mother. You have no idea how empty it feels to be without you …"

I can't help but smirk. "I think I might have an idea, Dad. It's okay." Despite the humor of the situation, I feel myself starting to tear up.

"Am I interrupting?" A feminine voice draws us out of our reverie. When we turn to the door, Grandmother and William are standing there, smiling at us.

15

Grandmother has a mug filled with a familiar-looking potion, and approaches the bed first.

"That's not what I think it is, is it?" Dad isn't a fan of Uncle Cyrus's weird medical brew. I don't blame him, the stuff works but it's disgusting.

Grandmother only smiles. "I think you know it is. I do apologize, but Mr. Salem insisted that I give this to you." As she hands Dad the mug, I stand up and go over to William, who offers a welcoming arm to hide under.

William … my boyfriend, my ally … for eighteen days, I only had our last kiss in Hawaii to keep me going in Hell. I'd nearly forgotten how good it feels to be in his embrace. My head naturally finds a path to lay on his chest as he cuddles me.

"How are you holding up?" His voice radiates his concern. I look up at him, my eyes captured by the newest feature of his face, a long scar that runs from his right eyebrow down to the bottom of his ear.

"Okay, I guess … I'm relieved to be back, and I'm so glad Dad's here for real … but still I can't quite shake the experience I had. It's going to be a while, I'm sorry."

William shakes his head. "No problem, Alanna, it's okay. I understand. Pele did say you might change after the journey …"

He sounds doubtful. I need to reassure him of one thing. "Don't worry, William." I reach a hand up to stroke his face. "I still love you." He smiles at the words, bowing his head slightly to kiss me.

Throat-clearing stops us before our lips can meet. Dad's throat-clearing. "Is there something I need to know about?"

We both look over to the bed, where Dad has probably the most humorous expression on his face I've seen in years. Clearly he's not mad, but he just needs to be filled in. With William's hand in both of mine, I pull him over to Dad's bedside, smiling right back.

"I suppose I should have told you about this earlier. Dad, this is William White Bear. William, meet the *real* Cole Sharpe."

William extends his free hand to Dad. "I'm honored, sir, to be in the presence of another Guardsman. Alanna has told me so much about you."

Dad chuckles. "That makes one of us." His voice takes a mildly scolding tone. "Alanna, when were you going to tell me about your boyfriend here?"

"Sorry, Dad, it never came up, what with the whole 'escape from Hell' thing."

"Well, I suppose I can forgive that." He looks back over to William. "She hasn't been too rough on you, has she?"

Now William's blushing. Dad managed to make a wendigo warrior blush ... how is that even possible? "Oh my, not at all, it's not like that ..."

"Relax, son, I'm joking. My little girl's got great taste." Dad raises his eyebrow slightly. "You seem familiar, actually ..."

"It's a long story," I interject. "I'll tell you more about it sometime."

Our reverie is once again interrupted, this time by Michika. We can't avoid the loud sound of her purring ... she's really taken to this cat form of hers. "Alanna, William, I hate to interrupt, but we need you out here. Gabe needs to talk with everybody."

17

I look over toward the door, scanning my best friend's appearance, trying to take in all of the changes. Her entire body is tiger-striped, her face has been lengthened and molded into a cat's muzzle, her eyes are bright yellow with almond-sliver pupils, her ears prick up and move around like a cat's, taking in all the room's sounds. Her bikini-top, her usual choice of shirt, seems so redundant now. There's even more contrast now between the rest of her body and the brown leather magic gauntlet she has permanently attached to her arm, which I now notice has been monogrammed with an enormous "M" at the top near her shoulder.

What's more urgent, though, is the expression on her face; abject worry. Michi never worries, and especially after her transformation she shouldn't be worrying. "What's wrong, Michi?"

She swallows hard. "He says we might be doomed."

Chapter Two: Family

July 5th, continued

There's decidedly more activity now in the main room of the house than there was earlier when I came in to see Dad. Supernaturals are milling about in greater numbers than I've ever seen before. Many of them are unfamiliar to me, which tells me they must have been recently rescued and brought to the Hidden-In-Plain-Sight Ranch. A few of them, however, are familiar faces.

One of those familiar faces is probably the only non-supernatural in the room, my grandfather Julian Vibria. He rushes over to me and hugs me tightly. "I'm so happy to see you back among the living, Alanna."

I return the hug gently. "Same here. It's been a long time."

Another pair of familiar faces, Teresa Iles and Trent Gracin, join the embrace. We're only interrupted when Gabe calls everyone to attention. Over the course of ten minutes, he outlines our exact situation with the Damnation Blade, along with the news that we'll likely be invaded by the New Empire within the year.

Too many of these people are already too frightened. How will they all fight?

Gabe seems oblivious to the worried rumblings of the group, and continues his speech. "We will need to mount a response to any attacks the SSA may launch at us. As we speak, Cyrus Salem is preparing a spell to allow us to stay one step ahead of the enemy, but it'll only be a matter of time before they figure out our

19

tactics and break them. As a result, we will be training you all to fight, effective immediately."

He motions for me to come to the front of the room. *Oh God, not now …*

"We have some good news, however, in that our forces will be joined by the Guardsman. Alanna Sharpe has returned from her long absence. She will be taking the lead in our defense."

Please, Gabe, don't promise things I can't deliver!

"Alanna, would you like to say a few words?"

I sigh deeply. As much as I'd like to tell Gabe off again, it won't do any good. I take his place in front of the crowd and clear my throat. "The SSA is powerful, but they are not infallible. We must be ready to rise to their challenge, to meet arms with arms, and to face our fears. I know none of you here, with very few exceptions, are soldiers. I know none of you here have ever had to fight before the New Empire came to power. With your help, though, we can bring the New Empire to an end. We can reclaim our rights, our humanity. We can change this world for the better, and bring peace."

A cheer starts from the center of the group, but it's not joined by many others. *Thanks for trying, Michi.*

Gabe clears his own throat to bring attention back to him. "We start training tomorrow. Those of you with any experience, either in the military or in police forces, you will be asked to assist in this effort. Let's make sure the battle waged against us is the last one the SSA ever undertakes."

With those words, the assemblage disbands. Gabe turns toward me, seemingly sensing my anger.

"Sorry about that, Alanna, I didn't mean to put you on the spot like that."

"I'm sure." I smirk at him. "So what's our plan now? I'm still minus a mother, you know."

"I understand that. Don't think that I'm not aware of your family's plight."

Laughter behind us interrupts the conversation. "Gabe, since when have you really cared about the Sharpe family?"

I look behind Gabe and see an old, wrinkly, yet familiar face. "Uncle Cyrus!" I rush over to the short wizard and hug him.

"We've missed you, child. You did well in the Inferno, we're all very proud of you." His words sound almost fatherly.

I hug him for a long time, then turn back toward Gabe. "Now, what does he mean by that remark?"

Gabe shrugs. Uncle Cyrus motions our attention back to himself. "The exact thing it sounds like. Gabe doesn't care about the bloodline that possesses the Sword, only that the Sword has a bearer every generation. This has been true as long as I've known you … as long as I've known Guardsmen, which is a really long time."

"Cyrus, you don't want to go here," Gabe warns.

"I *will* go here, Gabe, because you're about to throw poor Alanna here into the hornet's nest, so she deserves to be told up front what to expect!" Now the older man's voice sounds angry. I'm scared, even as his voice comes back to a normal level. "Alanna, unfortunately Gabe here has exactly one purpose to his existence, and that's to ensure the Sword is passed along to the next Sharpe to hold it. That's why he was the one to give it to you, and why he's been with you."

"It's more than that!" Gabe sounds agitated. *He's never like that!* "Don't you think I hurt every time a Guardsman perishes? Didn't I try to help the next generation? Didn't I offer counsel, offer support, offer sympathy? I think you horribly oversimplify my role here."

They're going at it pretty strongly. Maybe it's a good idea for me to withdraw, which I do, going back out of the room. To my surprise, as I go down the hallway I spot Dad, being supported by Grandmother, standing up and trying to walk toward me.

"Take it easy, Cole, you haven't walked on these in a while …"

"I feel fine, don't worry about me." He tries to let go of Grandmother's shoulders. "Did I hear Gabe right? The New Empire's trying to find this place?"

I nod solemnly. "Uncle Cyrus is planning some sort of defense, but I don't know what it is, or how it will help."

"It's good that he's doing that, but we need to do other things, little girl."

We're on the same wavelength, I think. "We need to find Mom."

"Exactly." He looks past me down the hallway. "We need to talk with those two down there."

I turn around and spot Teresa and Trent, in a private conversation. "Why?"

"They know Scolar's last schedule. I think it's going to come in handy, because I have a feeling Scolar knew where you mom is."

My heart jumps. "We can find Mom?"

"Maybe. It depends on what I find out." He holds out his arm to me. "Help out your poor old dad, honey?"

I can't help but smile and loop his arm around my shoulders. My own arm wraps around his waist, and slowly we make our way down the hall toward Teresa and Trent. When we get there, the two of them are very surprised by our appearance.

"General Scolar?" Teresa asks hesitantly.

"Once I was," Dad replies. "Now I need your help. I understand you two were with Scolar during his last detail, am I right?"

Trent nods. "What do you need to know?"

"I need to know what his schedule was. What did he have planned?"

Trent looks over to me questioningly, his roach-like face showing his confusion. "It's all right," I reassure him.

"Okay, well … after the MRZ, the General was to make a stop at Arlington, at the cemetery. Some sort of official business, he had no details. After that, he was returning to Washington for meetings with Vice President Regent."

Dad smiles. "Thank you, young man." He turns back toward me and whispers. "Your mom is as good as rescued."

He's smiling … genuinely smiling.

July 6th

I'm still not quite sure how this works, but Dad tried to explain it to me yesterday. While trapped in the Inferno, Dad had a few times when he came back to his own body, albeit for very short periods of time. During those times, he tried to leave clues for himself and for anyone looking for him, to try to help in his rescue.

The conversation continues this morning, as we eat breakfast. I have to admit, Dad's looking a lot better today … his body's filling back out, he looks more wide-eyed and stronger.

Like the Daddy I remember.

"So what I don't understand," I begin while gnawing on another bison cutlet, "is why you even had the opportunity to come back in the first place. I thought Scolar was completely in control."

"He was," Dad intones, "but that control came with a price. I'm sure you're learning as you go along, any kind of power has to come at a cost. In his case, he had to 'refuel,' so to speak, about once every couple of months. To do that, he returned to the Inferno, back to the place in Judecca where you found me. Those were the times when I was returned to my body."

"Did anyone else know about this?"

"For sure Jennifer Regent knew, because every time I had a Vice Presidentially-ordered armed guard around me, with orders to keep me in one place, or at least within sight."

Something occurs to me … "Dad, three years ago Gabe found a security camera video from Wisconsin which showed you in a rest stop bathroom."

Dad smiles. "One of my little breadcrumbs. I was hoping someone like Gabe would find that, and understand that I was being held against my will. Fortunately enough, he got it to you."

He also prevented me from killing you twice. "Are there other breadcrumbs to find?"

24

"There are, in fact I left them all over the country. As a matter of fact, Trent and Teresa were one of them."

"That's right … they were stationed at Flagstaff, weren't they?"

"Correct. They were intended to be a message to you, to let you know that I still called a few of the shots with my own body."

"So that means you knew … you knew that we could remove the control chips?"

Dad nods. "They tried to put one in me when they first captured me." He taps the right side of his forehead, the place where many of the rescued SSA supernaturals had control microchips implanted to brainwash them.

Now I have to know for sure. "Dad, what exactly happened in New Mexico?"

He sighs deeply. "I suppose the first thing I should do is apologize. I'm sorry I didn't tell you and Mom that I was freelancing for Gabe."

"It's okay, Dad, it doesn't matter now."

"Oh, I'm afraid it *does* matter, because if not for that we wouldn't have even gotten in this mess in the first place." He sets down his fork, takes a long slug from his coffee mug, then continues. "I got the call from Gabe on a Friday, just like all the others, complete with my cover story: the firm was sending me to do an on-location site survey.

"I remember kissing both you and your mother good-bye, and then flying over to Santa Fe. Gabe was there, and gave me the briefing. Some kind of supernatural activity was detected in a cave near Trinity Site, of unknown origin, suspected to be demonic. I could feel the energy from the place as I walked into the mouth of the cave, and so I kept the Sword in my grip.

"The activity in the cave was more frightening than I'd imagined. There was an entire army massing, equipment and men training. I don't think the United States Army had better-trained camps than this place. At the front of it was the Regents, they were consulting with some of the folks in charge. I realized then that the demonic energy wave seemed to be coming from them directly.

"Before I could do anything else, one of their lookouts spotted me. I drew the Sword and entered the battle. I made my way about halfway across the compound before I was overwhelmed and overrun by their superior numbers ... because after all, I was one soldier going up against an entire army. They subdued me, pinned me down. To my surprise, they were able to wrench the Sword out of my grip. When the migraine hit, I was too weakened to fight back, and one of them knocked me over the head with a rifle butt to knock me out.

"When I awakened, I was lying in a sterile environment, on an operating table. My arms and legs were strapped down, to prevent escape. There was a surgeon standing over my head, all I could see was his eyes and they were panicked. He looked away from me and said he couldn't get a chip into my head, because it wouldn't install, or initialize, or something. Hard-headedness is what I blame, it runs in the family."

I chuckle at Dad's joke, even as I'm more and more horrified by the story.

"Anyway, he told someone I couldn't see that he couldn't put a chip in me. A lady's voice replied that she had a backup plan. You can probably guess that it was Jennifer Regent who was standing there with us.

"She made her way over to the table, and glared into my eyes. I've never seen any woman as angry as she was in my life, not even when I've pissed off your mother to the point that she tries to cook me. She glared at me, then she slapped me hard across the face. I'll never forget the words she followed that with.

"'Your bitch is next, dog. For my brother.'

"I felt something being shoved into my hand, still pinned down. It felt cold and metallic, like the Sword, only less welcoming. As it turns out, she was shoving the Sabre into my grip.

"The instant she wrapped my fingers around the hilt, I felt infinite agony. My guts felt like they were boiling and freezing all at once. My teeth felt like they were peeling backward. I felt myself implode. With the last of my consciousness, I heard the sheath of the Sabre being removed.

"The next thing I experienced was torture. I was frozen into the ice pillar in Judecca. My arms and one leg were wrenched behind my back, and I couldn't move them. I was constantly feeling my tendons and muscles being ripped apart from that unnatural posture. It was only the first time that Scolar had to 'recharge' that I understood what was happening to me, and starting from the second I planned my escape by leaving the clues."

I don't even think I've been breathing as he's been telling me this story. I gasp a shocked inhalation, then clutch Dad tight in my arms. He's literally been through Hell, through an experience that I can't imagine.

And yet somehow I can.

"I'm so sorry that I lied to you, to your mom. I'm so sorry, if I hadn't done that … if I'd been up-front with you guys, then maybe this whole sorry mess wouldn't have happened, maybe the New Empire wouldn't exist, maybe Scolar would never have tormented you …"

He's nearly weeping. I'm already there. I clutch him tighter. "It's okay, Daddy. It's okay. I forgive you. You only thought you were doing what was right, and you didn't want to worry us. I can understand that, considering."

He sighs. "You don't understand, Alanna. Because of what I did, because I kept freelancing for Gabe, we might have delivered the world to Hell."

That's a disturbing thought. "But now you're back, Dad. Now you can fight it." I lift the Sword up from where it's been hanging off my hip. "You can take back the Sword and fight again."

He shakes his head. "I'm sorry, Alanna, but once a Sharpe generation claims the Sword, it can't go backward. You're the Guardsman now. I'm just a wreck of a man."

Someone taps on my shoulder, making me jump about a mile. I turn around, and my mood instantly sours. "What the hell do you want, Gabe?"

The agent raises his hands defensively, much like he did when he met me in San Antonio two years ago. "Whoa, Alanna, I mean no disrespect. I just wanted to interject into your conversation."

That's not disrespect? I don't get a chance to reply before Dad does. "What is it about?"

"The Guardsman. Specifically, how I can help you in particular, Cole."

Chapter Three: Penance

July 6th, continued

Gabe leads us into the darkened workshop of the Ranch house, the place where, three years ago, I watched Uncle Cyrus restore a gauntlet that had been buried in the ground, one which allows Michi to use magic. It looks like it's seen better days: there's scorch marks on the door and a lot of the timbers, clearly where a fight's taken place, and one window has been blasted into oblivion. Despite the summer air, I feel chilly as I follow Dad inside.

Gabe turns on the light, bathing us in all the glory a single 40-watt light bulb can generate. Once my eyes adjust to the darkness, I see a long shape, hidden under a dirty canvas rag, lying on the workbench.

Dad seems apprehensive. "I don't like this."

"Me either," I whisper to him. My voice is louder as I call to Gabe. "Why are we here?"

"I have something for your father, Alanna. You recall that two years ago, you effectively killed the Invader at the MRZ."

How can I forget? That day pops up in my nightmares from time to time … *the Missouri Rad Zone, held at bay on the other side of a massive wall … the Sabre raised in the air, the Invader ready to cut down a weakened Michi at his feet … me with a broken arm, barely able to hold the Sword in two hands … the shattering impact as Sword and Sabre made contact, sending shards of the Sabre in all directions.* Though it was a good day, it's still sickening to think if I had been weaker, or slower, that Michi would be dead.

"You don't have to remind me, Gabe."

Gabe has that maddening smirk on his face again. "Well, what you don't know is that I asked our inside connection at the MRZ to collect the pieces. While you were in Hell, I asked Mr. Lonstein to deliver them to me."

My blood chills at these words. "Gabe, why?"

"I wanted to study it."

Dad seems perturbed now. "What needs to be studied? It was made in Hell, it was destroyed on earth, seems pretty simple to me."

"I wanted to see if I could change it."

Now I'm really lost. "Why? To what end?" My voice is getting more and more agitated.

Gabe turns around to face both of us. "When the final battle takes place … and it *will,* don't think otherwise … I wanted to be prepared to face the New Empire on equal footing. Equal in terms of the New Empire anyway."

Dad starts chuckling. I don't find this funny at all. "In other words, you want *us* to have the unfair advantage, as opposed to *them.*"

"Precisely. The blade was a total loss, but there was a hilt. I figured that by changing the makeup of the blade's content … by forging it with a similar metal source to that of the Sword … then we could have *two* Guardsmen."

I don't claim to know a lot about metallurgy, but I'm still lost. My eyes drift down to the Sword, my new security blanket, comfortably hanging off of my right hip. I put a hand on the end of the hilt, resting it there, really.

"So … ?" Dad urges.

"So what?"

"So, will we have two Guardsmen or not?"

Gabe smirks again. "You tell me." And he pulls the canvas off of the lump on the workbench.

My heart drops, as that familiar Sabre lies there, in what appears to be a new leather scabbard. All the same, though, it's different. The dark aura that usually permeates the Sabre is noticeably missing, and I have no compulsion in any direction toward this weapon. As my eyes travel to the hilt, the finger guard has been changed, as well; instead of the gothic cross that had been there before, now there's only a familiar inscription, familiar because it's identical to the one on the Sword.

The family name.

SHARPE.

"Cole, much like the Sword was forged for your ancestor from the soil of the Holy Land, this one is forged from the soil of an equally pure place."

Dad looks at Gabe questioningly, but I blurt out the first thing that comes to my mind. "Avalon?"

"Yes, Alanna. Cyrus was kind enough to gather enough Avalonian soil to form a suitable blade. The purifying effect, combined with a couple of spells and a blessing from the Lady of the Lake, served to purge the last of the hellish influence over this Sabre. It's now fully on our side." He picks up the Sabre and holds it out before Dad. "Cole, this Sabre is now yours, to serve the Sword's Master, to serve life."

Dad hesitantly reaches his hands out to take the weapon from Gabe. I watch all of Dad's muscles tense up as he firms up his grip. He looks nervous. I don't blame him, he's probably afraid of Scolar coming back from oblivion to possess him again.

"Granted, I don't know what's going to happen when you draw it. It'll be another knight, I know that for sure. Without seeing him, I've taken the liberty of naming him."

Dad looks over at me, knitting his fingers into the hilt and clutching the Sabre tightly. His other hand grips the scabbard and pulls it off. In a brilliant flash of light, armor closes around him.

The armor looks like it's both dark and light, in equal measure. It almost looks like the Invader's armor, but at the same time elements of the Guardsman are evident. The shoulder guards don't display the New Empire sigil, nor do they display the Stars and Stripes like the Guardswoman's; it appears to be the family's crest with a pair of dragon wings added to it. The familiar family creed … *Ut Dei miles resurrectionis fortis contra infernum …* is proudly engraved around the crest on the left shoulder. On the right is the translated creed, "As God's soldier I rise, strong in the face of Hell."

Most reassuringly, though, the helmet has no traces of the death's head that marked the Invader. Just Dad's eyes, his loving, caring eyes, looking toward me. Gabe steps out from behind the newborn paladin, smiling.

"Alanna, let me introduce you to the Penitent."

The Penitent lowers his eyes and kneels before me, his Sabre held blade-down before him, edge pointed away from me.

An impulsive urge overcomes me. I draw the Sword. The Guardswoman's armor closes around me completely for the first time since before the Inferno. It's a comfort, warm and familiar. The best part, though, is the lack of an impulse to attack the bearer of the Sabre.

The Sword recognizes an ally.

I lift the Sword toward the Penitent … toward Dad … and lay the flat of the blade gently upon each of his shoulders. He lowers his head.

I dub thee Penitent, knight-errant in service to God Almighty. May we forever serve in His stead.

I sheathe the Sword, backing away. The Penitent rises to his feet and sheathes the Sabre, bringing Dad back out. He looks like he's had a religious experience.

Tears run down his face. "I'm whole again."

I rush up to Dad and hug him for a long time. Even once we're aware of Gabe leaving us alone in the workshop, we keep clutching to each other.

Father and daughter, knights of life.

Chapter Four: Breadcrumbs

July 8th

My energy level is back to what it was. I'm raring to go now.

I'm finally through with playing two years' worth of catch-up. I took some time the last couple of days to personally meet some of the other supernaturals around the Ranch that I didn't know, which revealed to me some interesting, potentially military-ready abilities. A lot of these folks have supernatural powers that could be used as potential weapons … weapons that the New Empire may not have any defense for. From what I've seen, the SSA prepares like a conventional military unit, using conventional military tactics and weapons. They're not prepared for gas attacks, for electrical attacks, for seismic attacks, or for anything remotely related to magic.

We have all four in spades on our side.

Michi is probably our best magical weapon, being able to access powers from both her gauntlet and her new status as Durga's servant. We spent a "girls' night in" last night, catching up over ice cream and firelight. I finally got her side of the story Aunt Kitty told me.

"I'm sorry about Mom, she's still kind of bitter about the whole situation," she told me. "What happened was I took what should have been a fatal injury from an SSA rifle, square in the chest. When Durga made me her servant, it saved my life." She pulled her new tail up into her arms, cuddling it to her. "I don't know what Mom's so mad about, this is pretty cool. Plus, I don't get nearly as wiped out when I use the gauntlet anymore."

She flexed her left arm, and I could hear the leather stretch and pop. She seemed very happy about it. I simply reached one of my hands out to her right hand, feeling the fur coating it entirely.

"I'm just glad to be back with you guys. Especially here."

She grinned at me then, her new, animalistic, fanged smile. "BFF's to the end."

"To the end, Michi. I promise."

Hugging my best friend never felt as good as it did last night. Today, though, I've spent focusing on preparing for the next stage of my quest. I'm packing up a backpack in my room when a familiar giant shadow passes over me.

"Your dad told me I'd find you here." William's deep voice makes me relax.

"Yeah … I figured we'll probably be leaving sometime soon, so I should be prepared." I turn around to see him. He has a mug of tea for me, which he hands over. "Thanks. So what's up?"

He smiles a little bashfully. "We haven't had a lot of time to sit and talk since you got back. I was hoping for a chance."

So have I, believe me. I motion for him to sit on the bed. I place myself right next to him, leaning against him, my thigh against his. His scar is the first thing I see when I turn my face to look up at his. My fingers find it and gently stroke it. "How did this happen?" I finally find myself asking.

He sighs. "It's a long story, Alanna."

I put my hand on his. "I've got the time. I want to know, anyway, just on general principle, what with being your girlfriend and all."

He smiles at that. "I suppose you're right." His arm curls around my shoulders. "I'm guessing you've already heard a lot about the battle that led to Michika being the way she is."

I nod. "I've heard about it from both Michi and Aunt Kitty."

"Well … while that drama was going on, I was on the far side of the Ranch house. There was an SSA contingent with some kind of new, giant weapon with rotating saw blades. I brought out the wendigo, cut through their numbers, ate a few of them, and finally got to the machine. As I was ripping out its heart, one of the blades caught the side of the wendigo's face. I finished destroying the weapon, turned back to the soldiers, and they all scattered. When they were gone, I pulled the wendigo back and found that my face was bleeding."

My fingers trace the scar. "You poor thing." Playfully, I reach up and kiss the scar gently.

"Thanks," he responds, smiling. "Grandmother did her best to stitch it up, but the damage was already done, and this is the result. Even after one of Cyrus's healing potions, this was the best that could be done, and from what I've been told it's because it's the wendigo's injury, not mine." He sighs heavily. "Another time now that the creature has ruined my life."

Now that doesn't sound like William. "What do you mean?"

He takes my hand in his, still against his face. "Alanna, the wendigo is a terrible burden to bear. Every time I let him out, I feel like I'm losing more and more of my humanity. It's a tenuous grip I have, and I feel it slipping more and more."

I take a deep breath. "While I was down in the Inferno, I felt the same thing. I felt like I was losing myself."

Now it's William's turn to look to me with concern. "What happened?"

I haven't talked about this with anyone. I'm afraid to. *Especially with William ... what if he stops loving me because of it?* "I had a guide down there, and he led me through the entirety of Hell to find Dad. While I was there, they made me do things ... terrible things ... I witnessed so much misery, punishment, torture ... I started participating in it."

William's face darkens.

"I tormented souls while I was down there. Some of them were by accident, because I couldn't avoid them, but others ... others I joined in their punishments, and I ... I *enjoyed* it ..."

I can't go on. I shrink away from my boyfriend, so afraid of his judgment. William sits there still.

"I'm sorry, William, it did change me. I'm a horrible person ... I had visions, too, terrible visions ... visions of losing love ..."

I'm getting inconsolable. My face hides in my arms, in my little ball of misery. I don't hear a word come from William.

Instead, I feel his reaction. He wraps his arms around me. He tightens his grip. His lips are on my forehead.

"Don't cry, Alanna, don't be sad. You're not a bad person."

I can't quite understand this. I look up at the man, and see his warm, smiling face. "But why not? You don't know …"

"I know you. I know a young woman, one who loves her family dearly. A woman who is willing to pay any cost to reunite them. A hero. She puts others above herself always. She wants to bring peace to the world in her way, she wants to restore the rule of order and common sense. She also is a wonderful friend.

"That's why I love her with all my heart." He takes my chin in his hand, lifting my face to his. "And I always will, beyond eternity."

His lips are on mine. I can't help but to return the kiss, the pent-up emotions being released all at once. My arms clutch around his neck. He pulls me into his embrace. Never once do our lips separate. It feels like an eternity in the most wonderful paradise I can ever know.

This is what I want, forever.

When we finally have to let each other's face go, he's managed to make me smile. My voice is but a whisper. "I love you too, William." My head makes its way to his chest. "Stay with me tonight."

"I will."

I finish packing my bag, filled to bursting with everything I think I'll need for the journey. All the while, though, I'm yawning. Sleep is starting to overcome me. William gently leads me to my bed and tucks me in. The cushion beneath me is relaxing, comforting; it feels like home.

My heart jumps as I feel motion behind me, lifting the blanket, then a warm presence completely against my back. *William. He's cuddling me.* My body relaxes even more. I bring one of his hands around to my face and kiss it gently before I drift fully to sleep, the best comforter in the world wrapped around me.

July 9th

William is still wrapped around me as I rouse this morning, slowly sliding out from under the blanket, the familiar mountain lion head keeping watch over the two of us. After a quick trip to the bathroom, I lean over his prone body and kiss his cheek gently to awaken him.

"Good morning, sleeping handsome."

His eyes flutter open. He turns to see my smiling face close to his, and reaches his face up to mine, to return the kiss. "Good morning yourself. What time is it?"

"About eight. I'm about to head down for breakfast."

William pulls the blanket off of himself, rising to a seated position on the edge of the bed. "I'll join you, I'm starving."

He's shirtless. My thoughts drift away from the quest very briefly as I ponder the sight before me. He stretches, then reaches for his shirt and pulls it on. I file the image deep in my mind where I can come back to it, and approach him to take his hand. He stands up, laces his fingers through mine, and together we walk down the hallway to the dining room.

Everyone else is awake by the time we get there. Michi, plowing into a double-sized breakfast, grins up at me. Dad is across the table from her, eating a bowl of oatmeal. Aunt Kitty is next to him, eating an egg and occasionally casting tired expressions toward Michi.

At the head of the table is Gabe, the only thing in front of him being a gallon-sized pot of coffee, which he pours mugs of from time to time. *You'd think he'd just pound it down straight from the spout!*

"Alanna, good morning. Now that we're all here, we can get this started."

I grab two plates of food and bring them to the table, one for me and one for William. "What are we getting started?" My question seems very quiet amidst the bustling activity around us.

Dad turns toward me. "We're planning our next move. We've got two more people we're waiting on …"

Just as Dad says that, Teresa and Trent come up to the table. "Sorry we're late, sir, we overslept." Teresa's apology seems very nervous, as she accidentally uses her ice powers and breathes a line of frost across the party.

"Not at all, please have a seat, guys." They both sit down, and Dad continues. "As I was saying, we need to follow some of my breadcrumbs, because at the end of the trail is probably going to be Ariel."

Mom. I haven't seen you in three years, not since the SSA took you away. We're so close to rescuing you.

Gabe's voice knocks me out of my brief reverie. "How do you know the SSA didn't find them?"

Dad smirks. "I hid them really well. Nobody's going to think to look where I left at least one."

I take a bite of bison steak and chew on it thoughtfully. Michi, however, slurps down two eggs before responding. "So the video Gabe gave us was one of them?"

Dad nods. "Every one had a message. Each was trying to tell you something. That tape was to show you I was still alive. Trent and Teresa, you were one of the breadcrumbs, to show that I still had some control at certain points."

"Yeah, about that," Trent pipes up. "I'm not sure I like that we were used that way."

"Trent," Teresa admonishes, "don't get too mad at Mr. Sharpe. He was in a desperate way, and besides he got us away from the SSA. We should be thanking him, not accusing him."

Trent grumbles slightly. Gabe seems to detect a situation that needs defusing, and stands up, coffee mug in hand. "Arguing does us no good right now. We need to coordinate our actions."

Dad nods. "Trent, if you will."

Trent nods, pulling out a sheet of paper. "I wrote down everything I could remember about General Scolar's itinerary. I don't know how much it'll help you."

The schedule rests at the center of the table. All of us stand up to look over its handwritten contents.

8 February -14 February: Inspection at MRZ, meetings with WO Lonstein, investigate disappearances from duty.

15 February: Attend Arlington maneuvers.

23 February: Meeting with SSA commanders, Langley.

25 February: Meeting with SSA investigators, Quantico.

28 February - 4 March: Meetings with Vice President Regent, honor guard for President Regent at UN Supernatural Summit in Washington.

I stroke my chin. "I never heard about this summit."

"It was a secret summit," Trent answers. "Only a few people in the General's inner circle in the SSA knew about it. They were planning to take the SSA worldwide back then."

Dad seems very intently focused on the schedule. "Did Scolar tell you exactly what these 'Arlington maneuvers' were?"

Trent shakes his head. "I never bothered asking. I assumed it was something having to do with the cemetery."

"Something else that's weird," William pipes up, "is that there's an eight-day gap after that listing. What was Scolar planning for those eight days?"

"Or was it you, Dad?"

Dad's got his eyes shut tight, like he's trying to think. "I don't remember. My memory's been really fuzzy about certain things … unfortunately this is one of those things."

I pull the schedule toward where me, Michi, and William are sitting. It's a ponderous thing, why this massive gap in time? I'm lost in thought when Michi pipes up. "Maybe you thought you needed eight days to rescue Aunt Ariel?"

Dad's eyes fly open and light up. "You might be right. Something's at Arlington that I needed to

43

retrieve … that's the 'maneuvers,' I need to get to the cemetery."

Gabe sighs deeply. "It's not going to be easy to travel. For starters, I'm not even sure right now where we are …"

"Outside of Edmonton," a voice chirps behind us. Uncle Cyrus is approaching the table with his own mug.

"Okay, thanks. So let's figure about three days' worth of driving to get to Arlington. Three days' worth of driving through hostile New Empire territory, dealing with checkpoints and armed patrols, and ducking around a lot of SSA agents which all have Alanna's photo on a 'Wanted Dead Or Alive' poster. We need to be stealthy, or we need to make a splash and attack everybody that we meet. It's going to be really difficult to get there, in other words."

I clear my throat. "What if we fly there?" To emphasize my point, I unfurl my wings.

Dad has a thoughtful expression. "It's a thought, Gabe."

Gabe has the same expression. "Maybe, but it's a long haul. Can you manage it?"

I nod quickly. "I flew a few times in the Inferno. If I can do that, with no air currents to speak of, then a cross-continent flight won't be any trouble."

Gabe comes around the table to take one of my wings in his hands. "Then this is going to be your only defense between the group and the SSA. Are you prepared for that responsibility?"

I stand up and turn to face Gabe. "With all due respect … I was born to do this. This is my mom we're talking about. If there's even a microscopic chance of getting her out of the New Empire's grasp, then there's no extreme I *won't* go to."

There's no reaction for a second. Then Michi stands up. "I'm with you, Alanna."

William stands up behind me and places a hand on mine. "Me too."

Dad stands up as well. "I think we're in agreement here. Gabe, let's get this show on the road."

Source: Alanna Sharpe Sighted in New Empire, SSA Injured in Confrontation

by A. P. Staff
July 6th, 2031

MOUNT ST. HELENS, WASHINGTON—Sources from within the Supernatural Suppression Agency are reporting that the terror mastermind Alanna Sharpe was sighted and confronted in the crater of Mount St. Helens on July 3, only slightly over two months after President Regent declared war on her and her supernatural army.

The sources, who commented on the condition of anonymity because their information was not considered official, stated that Sharpe was sighted climbing out of the ashes which permanently coat the floor of the crater. A patrol from SSA Troop 299, based in Tacoma, confronted the wanted terrorist as she emerged from the ashes. It's unknown whether it was Sharpe or one of her associates which fought back, but the entire patrol was later treated for injuries inflicted by a supernatural attack.

One agent on the patrol described the attack as a "shockwave" that knocked all of the victims aside, some being thrown as far as two hundred yards from their original position. Another agent described Sharpe as looking "haggard, like she had just gone through some kind of war."

Alanna Sharpe, the face of the supernatural opposition to President Regent's New Empire of America, is Public Enemy #1 in the New Empire for her part in the July 2028 attack on Chicago which destroyed the Sears Tower and most of the downtown area. She is also suspected in the disappearance of SSA General Tyrelius Scolar, who disappeared near Kansas City in 2029.

Officials with the Regent administration had no comment on the reports from Mount St. Helens.

Chapter Five: Dragonfight

July 12th

It's been too long since I've done this. Am I ready?

The last three days have been spent preparing for our cross-country journey. Specifically, Uncle Cyrus and Gabe have been working on a transportation basket that I can wear as the dragon to carry everyone on my back. We all agreed to this plan; it is going to be far too difficult for me to fly if I have to worry about carrying everyone bareback, or holding them in my arms, and trying not to drop anyone.

This morning, I'm back at the workshop, where I've been invited by Uncle Cyrus to inspect the final product. It's impressive, to say the least. Somehow, Uncle Cyrus and Gabe were able to find the chassis from an old minivan, which they sliced the car frame off of and welded to a strap rig that looks almost like a gigantic backpack.

Which I suppose is what it is, after all.

"Well? What do you think?" Uncle Cyrus seems way too enthusiastic.

"It's perfect. I think that'll do nicely." I bend over and hug the short wizard. "Thank you."

"Don't thank us yet," Gabe interjects. "We still need to get this thing on you and make sure it's not going to interfere with your wings."

Too true. If I can't flap my wings, this whole enterprise will be pointless. My thoughts are interrupted, however, as the rest of the traveling party comes around.

"We're flying in *that?*" Michi groans. "Dad, couldn't you have gotten something a bit more stylish, like a Jeep or something?"

"We work with what we've got," Uncle Cyrus responds. He places a small item in my hand. "Here, you'll need this."

I open my hand up. What he's placed in it looks like a hearing aid. "What is it?"

"It's a communication device, so that the people in the van can talk to you en-route. You won't need a mike, but you'll need the speaker. Trust me on this."

I suppose he knows what he's doing, right? I plug the device into my ear. "Did you have this when you guys were flying with Mom?"

Uncle Cyrus shakes his head. "No, but we also didn't have an enclosed flying space, either. You do, so as such we need to compensate."

Dad places his hand on the van body. "You're sure about this, Cyrus?"

"Positive. Would I put you in danger needlessly?"

We all smirk at both Uncle Cyrus and Gabe, but I'm the only one who says anything. "Do you *really* want an answer to that?"

Dad and Michi chuckle. William comes up just then. "So how is this going to work?"

Gabe opens the sliding door of the van body. "First thing's first, everybody in that's going. You guys will have to get in first whenever this is used."

The others exchange questioning glances, but obediently climb into the van. Dad and Michi take the front seats, while William sits in the back. Gabe slams the door shut behind them.

"All right," Uncle Cyrus says as he turns toward me, "your turn."

I nod, removing the Sword from my waist and moving the strap to wrap it around my left forearm. I close my eyes and focus on my body.

It starts with my wings. They unfurl from their hiding place within my back. I almost fear that I won't be able to do it, after spending so long in the Inferno, but then horrible thoughts come to mind. *Dead supernaturals lying at my feet. Friends, lovers, family, all gone. Jennifer Regent, grinning at me, threatening me, claiming responsibility while torturing me ...*

My body begins to grow. Subtly at first, but more strenuous after a couple seconds, my muscles expand, my skeleton deforms, my neck and face lengthen. I'm breathing heavier and deeper as my lungs expand their size within my quickly-growing chest. My wings enlarge to the scale that my body does. From my back a tail begins to sprout and scurry away from the rest of my body, growing longer as I grow ever larger.

The transformation is finally complete. My voice turns into a constant growl, as I turn down and inspect my dragon body. Just like I remember it, gigantic and scaly. Initially I was afraid of this, afraid of giving up all the control I had been learning with the Guardswoman, but eventually I came to embrace this ability.

If I can use it to defy its creator, all the better.

I look back at where Uncle Cyrus and Gabe now look so tiny against the ground. A snort comes from my dragon snout, accompanied by a brief blast of fire, another part of my physical abilities sorely in need of exercise. I nod at the others.

"Excellent. Here goes." Uncle Cyrus makes motions toward the van, which is soon engulfed in a blue glow. It rises up off of the ground, the straps hanging slack. Sensing I'll need them out of the way, I extend my left arm and wing, around which the left strap of the van-pack loops. Once the strap is secured around my shoulder, out of the way of the wing's motion, the right strap separates into two pieces and wraps around the right shoulder, finally snapping and becoming an unbroken loop once more.

I move the straps slightly. *"Feels good."*

"Excellent. Cole, can you hear me?"

Dad's voice comes loud and clear in my ear. "I hear you. We're all ready back here. By the way, Alanna, we brought your pack with us, it's in here."

I smile, the dragon's maw turning the expression into something much more threatening than intended. I test my wings, and am satisfied that I'll be able to fly while wearing the van-pack. I turn back to Uncle Cyrus and Gabe and give them a salute.

"Godspeed, Alanna," Gabe calls up to me. "Find your mother."

"We're ready for you guys when you come home," Uncle Cyrus calls up to me.

I let out a dragon roar, a satisfying, cleansing cry. My wings flap gently, then harder, allowing me to lift up off of the ground. Accounting for the extra weight on my back, I need to flap a little harder than usual, but eventually I'm high above the Ranch grounds, and have a clear view of the city skyline of Edmonton, off to the north.

Dad's voice chirps in my ear. "Okay, Alanna, take a gentle path to the right. I'll tell you when to stop turning."

I begin forward flight, stroking my wings like a swimmer strokes her arms in the pool. I'm picking up speed, bearing slightly to the right. When Dad tells me I'm on a good path, I stop my gentle bank and speed up. Adrenaline is giving me even more speed than usual.

We're coming for you, Mom.

July 13th

The flight has been fairly smooth thus far. The extra weight hasn't been much trouble, and I've been nearly able to get up to the speeds I reached while flying from Montreal to San Antonio. It's also been nice to hear the conversations inside the van … Dad and Michi and William, all three have been taking spirited turns talking about topics of interest to them.

It gets more intriguing when the subject gets more gossipy. Dad started it, though, with one little innocent question. "So Michika, tell me, do you have a boyfriend yet like Alanna?"

A nervous chuckle came from Michi. "Maybe. I don't know if I still will, though … he had to go home a while back."

I can't help but smile … she's talking about Fahaian. To tell the truth, I've missed his presence too, but they were starting to get serious before I left and it's got to be killing her right now. *I remember how eighteen days away from William felt like I'd had my heart carved out of me …*

William fills in Dad. "She was with Prince Fahaian, but he's still in Jordan. He hasn't come back yet."

"I can imagine. It's a shame about King Fahai, and I'm sure his son's going to do him proud. Why are you worried, though?"

Michi sighs. "He left, and then this happened." I can only guess she's talking about her transformation. "What the hell kind of king is gonna want a queen that can disembowel him if he pisses her off?"

Dad chuckles lightly. "You know, your mom had a similar dilemma."

"Really?"

"Absolutely. By the time your dad met her, she was already a cat like you. Despite that, the feelings between them were too strong, despite the big disparity in their personalities. They fell in love. Your mom even saved your dad's life more than once, including a time she brought him back from death."

"How did she do that?"

Dad clears his throat. "You might want to ask her, it's a personal thing and I'm not sure she'd want me telling you about it. Suffice to say, if she *hadn't* been in a cat body, she wouldn't have been able to do it."

My eyes scan the horizon as I listen to the conversations in the van-pack, looking for trouble. Unfortunately, I find it, far in the distance. I can't make out exactly what it is yet, but it's three airborne shapes, two small ones escorting a much larger one. I turn my head slightly back toward the pack. *"Heads up, we've got company!"*

I hear rustling in the earpiece, then Dad's voice pipes up. "I see them, bogeys about a mile off." Seatbelts click into place. "Alanna, do you trust me?"

What kind of question is that? *"Of course I do."*

"All right, no matter how crazy it sounds, if I give you an instruction on a direction to fly, you do it. Got me?"

"Sure, but how crazy are we talking?"

"We're talking dogfighting."

Oh God, he wants me to fight them! I almost protest, but then part of me remembers one vital thing about Dad: before he was the Guardsman, he was a fighter pilot.

The shapes approach faster. The larger one seems unusual compared to the other two. The smaller shapes, clearly escorts, are also obviously jets, small one-person cockpit aircraft armed with defensive weapons like machine guns. The larger shape has a weird flight path ... it's bobbing up and down, almost like ...

As the realization hits, I'm forced to duck a long ribbon of liquid fire, blasting from the large shape. *It's another dragon!*

Ducking the attack forces me into a barrel roll. Dad's voice in my ear is trying to calm me down. "It's okay, Alanna, take it easy. Breathe, sweetheart."

My heart is racing, but I do my best to calm down. *"What do I do?"*

"Don't worry right now about the escorts, they're going to be easier to pick off. I've got Michika on that. Keep avoiding the big guy's attacks, and when you get the chance give him some of your own."

I'm trusting him, but I feel like he's crazy. I hear the van's sliding door opening above me. My back muscles clench, awaiting the inevitable concussion attack that Michi loves to throw in fights.

She surprises me, though. *"ASTRAL BODY!"* That's one I haven't heard her use before, and I realize why when I see its effect: a meteorite drops out from above us and slams into one of the escort planes, turning it into a twisted metal fireball dropping toward the ground.

Remind me to thank her later for not blasting me with recoil.

"Hard left, Alanna!" Dad's voice breaks up my relief. I bank hard to my left, as another fire ribbon blasts underneath me, close enough that I can feel the heat scraping against my chest. I think he's close enough now. The churning begins deep in my stomach, crawling up my throat and into my mouth. I open my maw and let fly with my own firecast, much larger than my opponent's in terms of width and range. The other dragon does his own barrel roll to avoid my blast, but it's not nearly as graceful and I'm able to clip a wing.

The other dragon roars with animalistic fury and speeds up his wings, trying to charge me. As he approaches closer, I can see more detail about my opponent. He's a blue dragon, with a slightly wider wingspan than my own, and dark black eyes. Burned into the middle of his back and into his left arm is the New Empire sigil, the eagle and skyscraper logo that I've learned to hate for all they've done to me. My investigation doesn't last very long, though, as in mid-roll he opens up his mouth, planning to firecast again.

"Grab him, Alanna!"

Dad's right. This dragon's only strategy is to hit me with fire streams, which would be a sound strategy against an opponent that doesn't have fire of their own, or free will. I brace my shoulders and dig my own talons into his rear flanks, tearing into his scaly flesh. He roars and chokes on the fire he was about to shoot at me, flapping his wings hard trying to get away from me.

This draws the attention of the remaining escort jet, which makes a wide, circling turn and brings its guns to bear toward me. Bullets zing past, just barely missing the webs of my wings.

"Michika, get that guy!" Dad's voice sounds panicked.

"On it, Uncle Cole!" Michi, on the other hand, sounds confident. *"CONTRACTION!"*

The plane crumples up like it's made of so much construction paper. A newly-formed titanium boulder, it drops like the rock it's become out of the sky. Now all that's left is the dragon. He's managed to wriggle free of my grip, and now he's literally bleeding from his butt. He opens his mouth again. I can see flames forming at the back of his throat.

"Alanna, fire!"

I don't need Dad's cry to know what to do. Fortunately enough, I'm quicker than my opponent with my own fire … I think I've been doing it longer. The churning becomes a torrent, and I open my mouth and blast a long column of fire.

Right down the other dragon's throat.

The other dragon claws at his maw and the base of his neck, but the damage is already commencing. I circle and watch as holes begin opening in his hide, the result of being burned alive from the inside out. His wings stop flapping, and soon he's plummeting to the earth below, a fiery streak against the pure blue of the sky. I linger for a few seconds, then resume my own flight.

When I hear the van-pack's sliding door close again, I finally speak. *"Everyone okay up there?"*

"We're fine," Dad crackles in my ear. "Let's keep going. Just be aware, we might hit some more resistance, but hopefully nothing else like that."

"I hope not," I agree, but the question is already picking away at my mind. *Where did that dragon come from? Are there more of them?*

This smells like Gerard all over. My mind wanders back to Chicago, to my encounter with Dr. Benjamin Gerard, the monster who turned Mom into a dragon so many years ago, and who unleashed this form I'm in now and goaded me into rampaging through the city. If he's created one dragon, chances are he's created more …

My wings flap harder, faster, pushing me through the air at a blistering pace. I can't let up now.

Chapter Six: Respects

July 14th

My accelerated pace helped shorten the journey dramatically. As it turned out, the patrol we fought was the only one in that area of the Canada/New Empire border, and thus the only resistance we met. Seven hours later, I'm alighting to touch down in a forested area just to the west of Arlington.

The van-pack is a bit of a challenge to get off, since I have to work it around my wings, and I have to remove it without crushing the precious cargo inside. Uncle Cyrus only built the right strap with a release: the left strap is a solid piece welded to the underside of the van chassis. After some contortions of my dragon body, I'm finally able to get the pack off of me, setting it down upright, gently, on the mossy ground we've landed on. The sliding door opens up, and Dad, Michi, and William pile out. Meanwhile, I stand to one side and shrink back down into my human body. Once I'm down, Dad is kind enough to run up and cover me with a blanket.

"Sorry, William," Dad teases. "Can't have my baby girl running around naked."

It's true. Since I wrecked Mom's old uniform in the Inferno, my clothes are now a casualty if I grow into the dragon, so I'll need changes of clothes constantly if I continue to use that form. Michi tosses my bag over to me, from which I extract some underwear, jeans, a T-shirt, and a pair of moccasins, one of the few mementos I have of our home on the Navajo rez. Once dressed, I step back around the curtain Dad created with the blanket and rejoin the group, right at William's side.

"So where are we? I'm ready to find some butts to kick," Michi growls, cracking her knuckles.

"Well, we should be within walking distance of the cemetery." Dad steps away from the group briefly. "Yeah, it's through these trees. We'll need to go through the front entrance." He runs over to the van and pulls out another sack, in which are secured four Holographic Self-Image Projectors. "Put these on and power them up. We'll need them to get through undetected."

Each of us takes one of the wristwatch-like devices and straps it to an arm. Almost like we're on cue, all four of us power up the HoSIPs, which create camouflage bodies for us, so that we don't look like ourselves. In this case, we don't even look like anyone we know; they are set to random attributes, so we look like nondescript men and women.

Michi looks at her body and groans. "Man, what's the point of being a cat girl if I can't show off?"

"Showing off isn't going to do us any good," William intones, though I kind of see Michi's point because my boyfriend is now just a plain old slacker-looking man. Nobody's at least complained about mine or Dad's bodies, though, which I suppose is a good thing. Nondescript is going to save our lives on this trek.

"All right, bodies are on, let's head out. We'll come back here once we've finished." Dad starts striking out, and we're all hard-pressed to keep up. Eventually we reach the front gates of Arlington National Cemetery, after a too-brisk walk.

All four of us take on hushed tones to our voices and our steps as we cross into the grounds. The lines of white tombstones, stretching as far as we can see, are chilling and almost religious all at once. So many lives, given in the name of freedom, are laid to rest on these grounds.

When all is said and done, will we be joining them in the ground?

I cast a nervous glance back at the guards, just waiting for one of them to pull a weapon and stop us, but thankfully they're stock-stiff, staring out, persistently on guard, keeping these sleeping heroes safe. I catch up to Dad, who's urgently scanning through the headstones.

"What are we looking for?"

"Believe me, you'll know it." He keeps walking, mumbling numbers and letters to himself. Michi crouches down at one of the newer headstones, stroking the face of it gently. I come over to where she's paying her respects, and spot the name on the stone.

CDR. LEVON JEROME LAZARUS, USN

She looks up at me. "Grandpa. I didn't know he was here." She turns sadly to the name again. "I remember we had to go to Japan for his funeral, but I didn't know they transported him here to lay him to rest."

I put a hand on Michi's shoulder. "I'm sorry. I know you and your mom loved him a lot."

She wipes a tear away from her face, creating a brief shimmer in her camouflage body. I can see the true Michi through it, see the sadness on her cat face. "I love you, Grandpa." She places a light kiss on the stone, just above the name.

"Guys, come on! We're close!" Dad calls over to us, with William at his side. I help Michi back to her feet, then we jog over. Once we're regrouped, we only move over two more stones before we're stopped by Dad.

He kneels down and lowers his face. I kneel down next to him and look up at the headstone, reading the name.

CDR. KENNETH RICHARD SHARPE, USN

"In this plot lies the last Guardsman before me, my father."

Dad's words sound so solemn. Then again, I suppose they should be, since it's my other grandfather. I'm so used to Julian now, I sometimes forget that I had another set of grandparents.

Dad's face takes on a dark shadow. I take his hand. "Dad? What's wrong?"

He smirks and turns back to me. "It's funny. I spent so long hating his guts. We spent years and years apart, never knowing where he was, only seeing him three days out of an entire calendar year. Mom died while he was deployed, and he never knew. He never seemed to even care." He takes a shaky breath. "I hate to admit it, but if it wasn't for him leaving me the birthright … willing me his position on his old unit … you would have never been born, Alanna."

That's right, Dad met Mom by taking his father's place on their team. I squeeze Dad's hand. "Do you still hate him?"

He sighs deeply, then smiles, warmly and truly, at me. "Nah. I can't stay mad at him. He *is* family, after all, and your mom would never forgive me if I kept hating him." He pulls me into a gentle hug, but as he does I feel something hard under my knee.

That's weird, there's only grass here.

Dad senses my encounter when I flinch. "What is it?"

"I think there's something under my knee. It's kind of hard."

He puts his hand down where my knee is. Michi and William lean over us, giving us some cover from prying eyes. "I think we found it. Alanna, honey, I need you to scooch about three inches to your left."

I do as Dad asks, and he digs his fingers deeply into the grass where my knee had been resting. A large square of the sod lifts up almost too easily, which he folds over. Underneath the newly-formed divot is revealed a narrow metal box. I dig my hands down around the edges of the treasure and pry it out of the earth.

"This is it. You just found my best-hidden breadcrumb." Dad smiles and tousles my synth-hair. "I knew you'd be the one to do it, Alanna."

"Thanks, Dad." The box has a hinged lid and a latch. I unhook the latch and, with trembling fingers, open up the lid. Inside the box are a file folder and a plastic zipper bag. I take the file out of the box and open it. The first thing in the file is a note in Dad's handwriting.

To Whoever Finds This:

Contained in this file are top secret plans of the New Empire of America. These plans entail an experiment that should have been destroyed nearly twenty years ago, but has been restarted. If you are reading these words, then I leave it to you: you must destroy this project, at all cost. This project has cost me too much already. It has cost me a wife and a daughter. It cannot cost anyone else even one single life. Take this information to the press, release it online, do what you must to make sure this material sees the light of day.

Lt. Cdr. Cole Sharpe, USN (Ret)

I look up at Dad. "Do you remember writing this?" I show him the note.

"Vaguely." He's moved on to the plastic bag. I'm still checking out the file, which is overfilled with documents, diagrams, maps, and photographs. I scan through some of the documents, and the scientific jargon goes straight over my head—something about genetic markers, hormonal resettlement, and the like—but then the photos catch me.

Lines and lines and lines of dragons. They're curled up in glass tubes, which look kind of like wombs. All of them are similarly marked like the one that attacked us in mid-air, with the New Empire sigil branded into their right arms and their backs.

I need to know more. I'm suddenly feeling very exposed out here. "Dad, we need to go back to the van, so we can decide what to do."

"Looks like I already decided when I left this breadcrumb." He holds up the plastic bag, and shows me the contents. It's an entry badge for Scolar.

I narrow my eyes and read the text. "Experimental Military Laboratory … Patuxent River?"

My blood chills. Patuxent River holds a very harsh part of my family's history, the place where Mom was turned into a dragon, the place that employed Gerard. Dad's face, however, is cut in stone.

"You're right. Let's go." He takes large strides, and it's very difficult for the rest of us to keep up with him.

After a half hour, exactly fifteen minutes less than it took us to get to my Sharpe grandfather's grave, we're back at the van-pack, all four of us inside the vehicle's chassis. Dad cracks on a magic flare Uncle Cyrus packed for us in the glove compartment, so that we all have light as the sun sets, and we all collect around the middle of the passenger compartment.

"Alanna, open the file, let's see it."

I nod at Dad and spread out the paperwork I found in the file folder. The photos wind up near Michi, the diagrams and maps by William, while I wind up with the documentation. We all look through what's closest to us.

"Okay," Dad starts, "who wants to share first?"

Michi holds up a couple of the photos. "Here's what I see, a bunch of dragons being grown and harvested like a farm. I have no idea what the New Empire is doing with dragons."

Maybe you don't but I do. My face darkens, thinking back to Chicago, back to how I was framed as a terrorist.

"Okay, so how complete do they look?" Dad has continued while I've been fuming.

"Just about finished, actually. If they're the same age as the one we fought, they'll probably be ready to go in no time."

"Just what I thought," Dad confirms, grinding his teeth. "William, what have you got?"

"A map. Take a look." William spreads the map out between all four of us. "It looks like we're going to be facing an honest-to-the-Creator labyrinth. The entire lower level of the facility is made up of those pods, only broken up by guard offices. The upper level consists of three research laboratories, a holding cell, and living quarters for the staff."

Part of his description catches my attention. "A holding cell?"

"I think it's a holding cell, at least. There's a room that's marked 'living source,' which I think means they're holding a donor there." William looks over at me, his face showing his instant guilt over his word choice. "Oh no, I'm sorry, Alanna, I didn't mean …"

"No, no, it's okay, I understand." *If there's a "donor" being held, it's probably Mom.*

"Okay, good," Dad interjects. "That leaves us with the last of it. Alanna?"

I flip through the sheaf of papers. "Most of this is scientific jargon that's going way over my head, but there's one thing in particular that's interesting to me. The dragons are referred to as STBs, which is apparently an acronym for 'Supernatural Tactical Beast.' There was an order made about a year ago as of this paperwork for a quantity of 25,000 STBs in anticipation of something referred to as 'Operation Glass Jaw.'"

"Any details?"

"Nope. Just the name of the operation, there's nothing like details about what it is or where it's taking place."

"Well that's worrisome." Dad strokes his chin. "As far as the rest of the contents of the box, I showed it to you, it's apparently a badge that will get me into the facility. So now we have to decide what to do."

I think Dad's already made up his mind. He has that expression on his face, the one that he gets when he talks about going into battle with Mom. *He's going, no matter what.*

William clears his throat. "Well, we don't know what Operation Glass Jaw is, but if that name's any indication, it's an attempt to show some kind of weakness in its target. If the dragons are part of it, we should try to disrupt it."

"Sure," I answer. "The only problem is we need to know how far advanced these dragons are in their growth. Are they going to kill us as soon as we lift a finger on them? Are they trained at all?"

"How many does it say are complete?" Michi asks.

I flip through more pages, hoping for a small number. Unfortunately it doesn't come. "Out of the original order of 25,000, this says that about 3,850 are complete, in their final stages of growth. The only thing is we saw one of them on our way here, so God knows how accurate this is now."

Dad nods. "True, this is at least two years old. We need recent intelligence."

We're stuck with what we've got, though. We're going in blind, just like usual.

I take a deep breath. "Well, I think it's important enough to the New Empire that these dragons get deployed. I'd say that's as prime a target as any."

William raises his eyebrow. "Are you sure?"

I nod. "Between the four of us, I think we can handle nearly four thousand inexperienced, newborn dragons. If their combat skill level is anywhere close to that one we fought on our way here, it'll be a piece of cake." I smile to emphasize the point, but I'm not sure they're buying into my bravado.

Michi nods. "You're right. Let's do it. I say we go to the lab and fuck some shit up!"

"Well, we know whose kid *you* are," Dad jokes. "How about you, William, Alanna? Are you guys in on this?"

William shrugs. "If the wendigo can help …"

"It can, believe me." I reach across and take William's hand, turning to Dad. "You got us all."

Dad smiles. "Good. We'll rest tonight, then tomorrow we'll go to Pax River." He collects all of the contents of the metal box and puts it up in the front seat.

What did we just agree to do?

Chapter Seven: Shock and Awe

July 14th, continued

Darkness falls quickly in northern Virginia, even in the summer time. We start up a campfire outside of the van-pack, just trying to shine some light on our surroundings. The others take a lot of time to get comfortable, particularly William and Michi.

Michi's doing weird things, I notice. Every so often, her gauntleted hand waves over the campfire, and she closes her eyes. I see sparks arise from her fingers, but nothing ever comes of it. I sit down next to her.

"Damn, why doesn't it work?" She sounds frustrated.

"What are you trying to do?"

She looks over at me, a little bashful. "Well ... I was trying to get through to Fahaian. I suppose that if he can do anything with fire, communication would be a cinch for him."

A flaming phone. I chuckle slightly. "You really miss him, don't you?"

She curls her legs up under her chin. "Yeah. The day he left to take the throne, he promised he'd come back to me. He *promised* me. Doesn't a promise from a king mean more than a promise from anyone else?"

I wrap an arm around my furry best friend. "I suppose it does. But I also think a promise from someone you love means even more."

She nods sadly. "I think I really do love him, Alanna. I get jealous of you and William sometimes, just because you guys know for sure, y'know? You guys are a great couple."

I blush, though I don't know if she can tell in the firelight. "I didn't know for sure at the start, y'know. I wasn't even sure I could even *trust* him, if you remember."

She grins. "Like I didn't think we could trust Fahaian. Trust issues are a surefire matchmaking process, didn't you know that?"

We both laugh. It feels good, because there hasn't been much to laugh about lately. She waves her hand over the flames again, producing sparks but not much more. Her shoulders droop.

"Don't get down about it, Michi. He'll come back. I'm positive."

She sniffles and wipes an eye. "I hope so." She suddenly yawns.

I make a motion toward the van-pack with my head. "Go on and hit the sack. William already did."

She yawns again and stands up. "Are you coming?"

"In a bit," I answer, though my eyes are on a dark shape fairly distant from the camp, standing a silent vigil against the night. Michi smiles in understanding, climbing back in the van-pack. I stand up and make my way over to where Dad stands.

"It's colder here than I remember summer being," Dad mutters.

"That's your nerves, Dad, just like mine." I wrap an arm around his waist. "She's over there, isn't she?"

Dad nods sadly. "She's there, I'm positive. We need to get her out of there." He takes a deep breath, and when I look up I can see his cheeks glisten in the starlight.

"We'll get her back."

Dad looks down at me. "I'm sure we will, Alanna, I have no doubt. I just worry about what's happening to her right now. What those bastards are doing to her."

I squeeze his waist gently. "We'll find out, and we'll put a stop to it, one way or another. Mom's coming out of that place tomorrow."

Dad smiles again, a wan smile of resignation. "I wish I had your confidence, Alanna." He wraps his own arms around me. "I guess you get that from me, huh?"

It feels so good to have Daddy hug me again. "Maybe a little bit. I don't believe any situation is hopeless."

He clutches me tighter. "Even in Hell?"

"*Especially* in Hell. I knew I would find you eventually, I knew that we'd rescue you. Even if it killed me, I was going to get you out of there. Just like tomorrow, we're going to get Mom out."

He clutches me tighter, almost to the point I can't breathe, but I do return his embrace. "God, if I lost either one of you ... I don't know what I would do."

His voice doesn't sound as confident as mine. *I hope things go as planned tomorrow. Daddy can't lose now, not after all he's been through.*

July 15th

I've come to the decision that it'll be easier to put the van-pack on if I grow into the straps, rather than putting it on once I'm grown. After breakfast this morning, everyone else piles into the van while I climb underneath it and begin my transformation. My muscles strain against my clothes, eventually shredding them as the dragon emerges. To my relief, my calculations were correct, and the wings find their way out from underneath the van-pack. I secure the release on the right strap, and I'm ready to go.

"Stay low against the treetops. That'll fool radar. We need to get there quick and sneaky."

"Got it, Dad." I flap my wings and bring myself into the air again, only just as high as the trees grow. I resume my forward stroke with my wings and begin forward motion, relying on Dad to give me the direction to go.

Dad's advice to stay low works as we avoid any entanglements with New Empire patrols, eventually making our way to Maryland. The Patuxent River facility turns out to be a single hangar at an abandoned air base, cutting a menacing profile into the pavement. Even in my dragon form, I shudder at the thought of what's going on in the darkened building. A light rain starts falling as I alight and land in a clearing, a thicket hidden by a deep circle of trees close to the hangar.

I quickly and carefully remove the van-pack before shrinking back down. Once to my normal proportions and dressed again … outfit number two being history … I rejoin the group, HoSIPs strapped on. William, Michi and I still have randomized bodies, but Dad is able to scan the entry badge and create his own camouflage body.

My heart flutters as I see him approach with his HoSIP activated. There he stands once more, Scolar in all of his glory. Scars cross his face. The deep blue of the SSA uniform he wears emphasizes his pale complexion. It's frightening.

Calm down, girl. Scolar's destroyed. You did it yourself.

71

"Okay guys," Dad intones, "here's the plan. I'll take the point, get us in the facility. Once we're inside, we start with the dragons. Take out as many of them as possible. Then we'll move up to the second level and try to find anyone who needs rescuing. Got it?"

We rustle amongst ourselves and come to agreement. I clutch the Sword tightly to my hip, even though with the camouflage body it's invisible. The reassuring heft of the weapon is the only thing that's keeping me from running away from this adventure.

When I look over at Dad, I notice that he's clutching the Sabre tighter as well. *He's just as nervous.* "All right, let's go."

We allow Dad to lead us toward the front door of the hangar, which is only defended by a single keypad with a card scanner. The card slips easily through the slot, activating a green light. I pull open the door, allowing all of us through into the building.

We're not entirely prepared for what greets us, though. The photos did these pods no justice; they stretch from floor to ceiling, each of them containing a fetal-curled dragon, awaiting deployment. Although there's a lot of filled glass cylinders, there's also a lot of them that appear to only have liquid, or very small cellular materials.

Dragon embryos.

Dad immediately draws the Sabre, at the same time deactivating his HoSIP. The Penitent makes his appearance known by smashing his weapon into the nearest glass pod, skewering the dragon within it. As soon as he does, though, the other dragons in the other pods begin stirring, almost like they share the pain.

Like they know.

"What are we waiting for? Let's go!" Michi drops her HoSIP camouflage and points her gauntleted arm around at the glass pods, calling off spell after spell, shattering each of the pods. William's body bulks enormously and grows into the wendigo, reaching his arms out across the aisle and ripping into dragons and pods alike.

Fluid is starting to flood the passageway. Dad and the others seem to have this under control. I quietly slip out behind them and make my way to the end of the walk, to the only ladder in the place. I quickly ascend to the second floor.

Mom, I'm here.

It's dark on the second level. I don't think a light's been on up here in years. Cobwebs line the passageway, threatening to collect me in their sticky path. My eyes take on their dragon attributes, trying to cut through the gloom, but to no avail.

I keep a hand on the Sword, clutching tighter as I clear my path with my free hand. Clanging behind me makes me slow down and crouch against a wall. I don't know what or who's following me, but they're in for a nasty surprise …

A tap on my shoulder makes me shriek with surprise. It's Dad. "What do you think you're doing?" he stage whispers to me.

"The same thing I bet you're doing."

He smirks. "Let me handle this, Alanna, you go back downstairs and take out those dragons."

"Dad, we both need to go. If Mom's going to be rescued, it's going to be by her whole family, not just one or the other of us."

Sudden laughter interrupts our heated discussion, coming from the end of the passage. This so reminds me of another time, another place …

Traverse City.

"I see now, the Sharpe clan is complete!"

My teeth grind, and I growl. *Gerard!*

"Of course, you wouldn't know it, but you're going to be witnesses to the greatest victory the New Empire will ever claim." A shadow appears at the end of the passage, approaching us threateningly. It looks like Gerard, but it's different.

Bigger.

"What are you up to, Gerard?" Dad demands.

"You mean you don't know? Try to guess. Come on, I like having my work acknowledged!" He hasn't stopped approaching. I can almost see his teeth, see his manic grin.

I let out a loud, almost dragonish growl. "You're cloning Mom. Those dragons down there, they're shoddy copies of Mom's dragon. Is that the handiwork you're so proud of?"

Gerard seems to shake his head. "Oh my, but you're only half right. You should be happy, Alanna. I've given you a great gift!"

What?

Gerard comes into the dim light, and I realize that my assessment is totally wrong. His skin, his skeletal structure, all of it is changed. He's scaly. Blue scales.

Oh God, no …

"What? Don't you understand? Those aren't clones." His smile turns into a sinister sneer. *"They're your siblings!"*

74

Every organ in my body bottoms out. I start hyperventilating. My eyes are warm. *It's just like my nightmare in Circle 8 … Gerard and Mom …*

Rage overwhelms me, the memory refreshed of the horrifying dream. I draw the Sword, unfurl my wings, and rush the dragon doctor. My vision is blood red.

This rapist must die!

I'm barely conscious of Dad rushing behind me, the Penitent being loosed once more. Gerard seems prepared for this. He digs his feet into the walkway, hunches his shoulders, and opens his mouth. I can barely see the glimmer of a spark in the back of his throat.

A long column of fire spews forth from the monster, coating me. Black char forms on the surface of the armor. My eyes burn, but in my enraged state, I just don't care. I put the Sword in front of me, continuing on my path toward him.

He unfurls his wings and flaps gently, lifting up over my head. Landing behind me, I hear a thud as Gerard takes the Penitent out with a swift kick, followed by his arms wrapping around my neck. He's trying to rip the Guardswoman's helmet off of my head. His strength is unnatural, like he's concentrated a dragon's muscles completely into his human body.

I ram my elbow back into his midsection, but it doesn't faze him. He swings around and faces the Penitent, the motion so awkward that it forces me to drop the Sword. I shrink back down into myself, I feel the heat forming in his mouth again.

The Penitent sheathes his Sword, and Dad raises his hands. "Now, Gerard, stop. Let her go. This fight is between you and me."

"Oh no, no no no, this fight is between the entire Sharpe family and me. Your whore of a wife did this to me!" He points to the lines of four scars on his face while tightening his arm's grip around my throat. "She disfigured me! All she needed to do was come back to the facility, to do as she was ordered to do … but no, your daddy had to come along and screw me over!"

Dad grits his teeth. "You have a strange version of it, Gerard …"

"It's the true version!" He tightens his grip on my throat. He narrows his eyes at Dad. "I saw you and your party come in, by the way. Once my children below are finished with them, they'll be left alive … I want to take a careful examination of all of you. After all, won't the STBs be much more effective if they have *actual* supernatural genes?"

I'm clawing desperately at Gerard's arm, but he tightens more as I scratch harder. My head is starting to spin … my hearing is waving in and out … in one of the in moments, though, I catch one particular sentence coming from Gerard's foul mouth.

"… imagine a wendigo-dragon, a tiger-dragon, a tiger-wendigo … the possibilities are *endless!*"

Not William … Michi … Mom …

I let out a strangled roar, clutching tightly to Gerard's arm and trying to flip him over my head. He simply laughs, digging his newly taloned feet into the floor of the passage. "You silly little girl, what are you trying to accomplish?"

My fingers scrape against the Sword's hilt. "This, you bastard."

I clutch the Sword. As the Guardswoman emerges, I spin the weapon around to point the edge behind me and thrust it deeply into Gerard's abdomen. He lets out a primal scream of rage, firing off another wild firecast into the air, backing away from me.

"You little *bitch!*" He grits his teeth, unfurls his wings, and crouches down into a three-point stance. Flapping his wings, he charges me. In the meantime, Dad's already re-drawn the Sabre. Gerard approaches quickly … he's almost on top of me …

I hit the floor, watching as Gerard runs over me. His face shows an instant of surprise before he reaches the Penitent, who brings the Sabre down in one smooth chopping motion. The scientist's head rolls all the way down to the end of the passageway as his body stumbles and collapses.

Gerard's face initially shows shock. Then a manic grin. His eyes close. An alarm klaxon blares over our heads.

We both sheathe our weapons, turning back toward the other end of the walkway, intending to rush to its ending, but we're stopped by a yell from downstairs.

"Guys, get down here! We got a problem!" Michi's screech sounds more worried than I've ever been used to. We both scramble back down the stairs.

When we rejoin the group, I can instantly see Michi's problem. She and William are trying to stand their ground, but every cylinder that hasn't been wrecked by the two of them has been opened, unleashing every dragon in the place. Blue, green, scaly, big as life, they scrabble across each other, attacking whatever they see in a fit of rage.

Then several of them spot us.

Chapter Eight: The Last Dragons

July 16th

Midnight chimes far away from our location. The four of us frantically sprint out of the lab facility, followed by a wild bunch of enraged dragons, all writhing around and acting on instinct. We're not even sure how far away is going to be safe to turn around and face our opponents.

Dad finally turns around, his hand on the Sabre. My heart jumps. "Dad!"

"Keep going, guys! I got this!" He draws the Sabre, allowing the Penitent to rush into the battle.

William grabs my elbow. "He's not thinking straight, Alanna, he thinks he's going to find your mom if he's the one to attack."

I'm in complete agreement. My body is already straining.

If I'm going to fight dragons, it's going to be on an even battlefield.

My neck lengthens, my muscles bulk up, I let out a primal dragon roar. My wings flap hard, lifting me off the ground and sending me into the depths of the battle.

These dragons seem about as skilled as the one I fought with in the air, which is to say not very. They haven't had any training or experience using their abilities. Anything they do to fight back is all based on things that are imprinted on their primitive minds.

It's a good thing I know how to fight them, then. My talons rip through scaly flesh, shredding hides left and right. When I get the chance, I shoot fire down a couple of the dragons' throats and watch them burn up from the inside out. I bite into throats and rip them out. I rip through wings.

I'm taking damage just as well as the others are, though. I feel the webbing of my wings getting cut to ribbons … there's no way I'm flying out of this mess. I feel every purchase on my flesh, see the burn marks from every enemy firecast. My head stays in the battle, but I'm quickly losing my energy.

"CONCUSSION!" Michi's favorite spell blasts several of the dragons away from me. Now that I've been able to observe her, I've noticed that her spells are now extremely more powerful than they used to be. That might warrant some worry, but now isn't the time. Another wave of dragons approaches.

The wendigo races past, teeth bared, saliva glistening in the moonlight. He races into the battle and starts rending flesh of the dragons, and every once in a while I see his face getting coated with dragon blood, consuming his victims. I'd be a little worried about that as well, but …

I trust him.

I shoot off a fire stream through the middle of the dragons' numbers. I turn back to Michi. *"How many have we destroyed?"*

"Are you kidding? How the hell am I supposed to keep track? *CHASM!"* A fissure forms in the ground beneath us. The Penitent is nearly caught in the mess, but I catch him and pull him on my bloodied back. The crack appears to have lava at the bottom, and a huge number of the dragons are stumbling and falling to their doom below.

More dragons are scrambling toward us, but these ones are smart enough to jump or flap over the chasm that's been created in front of the doorway. Michi raises her hand, ready to power another spell. The wendigo hunches, ready to strike. The Penitent brings the Sabre to *en garde,* and I crouch and snarl at the oncoming horde.

An earth-shattering roar behind them stops their progress. We're all taken by surprise as a giant fire stream obliterates a good number of our dragon foes. The flames shimmer and make everything around them glow. We hear the growling approaching, and we're ready for another opponent.

Another dragon appears, a green one. This particular dragon is much larger than the ones we've been fighting ... much larger than I am even in my dragon form. There's smoke trailing up from its nostrils, and it snarls. To my surprise, it turns and starts fighting the other dragons ... and making very short work of them. They have no response to an opponent as skilled as this dragon is.

My adrenaline is starting to subside, and I'm now aware of some major differences, besides size, between this newcomer and the other dragons. The new dragon has no tail ... instead, there are fins on its forelegs. *Every once in a while, in the right light, it looks like it might have hair ...*

The dragon finally cuts through the final of the enemy dragons, then turns toward us. Its eyes ... or eye, rather, only one is visible ... glows bright red with rage. It opens its mouth, and I can see a fire stream starting up deep in its throat.

I need to act!

I leap across the chasm Michi created.

William, shrinking back from the wendigo, yells over to me. "What are you doing? Come back! It's going to destroy you!"

If my hunch is right, it's not going to.

The others are held back from me by Dad, who as the Penitent is holding the Sabre in front of my friends to keep them away from us.

The other dragon rages. It growls. It backs away from me. It wants to fight me, that much is clear, but it's conflicted.

I need to know for sure. I stand up on my haunches, and I extend one of my front talons toward the other dragon. "Mom?"

The dragon is instantly confused. It shrinks backward. It looks up at me questioningly.

"Mom, it's me. It's Alanna." To emphasize my point, I begin shrinking back down into my human form. I'm going to be naked, bloody, and bruised, but right now it's more important that this dragon realizes I really am who I say I am.

The dragon's eyes follow my shrinking body. An expression of recognition appears on its face. A rumbling comes from its throat, like it's about to either speak or spew fire. Once I'm fully human, I stand in front of the dragon with my hands spread out, to show I mean it no harm.

"Mom, it's me. It's really me."

The dragon's expression turns sad. It opens its mouth. "Alanna ..." It starts its own shrinking, slowly at first, but eventually at the same rate that my own took place. The process seems like it takes an eternity, until finally all that's before me is a woman, kneeling

81

in the darkness, her head down. Just as slowly, the figure stands up.

My heart is in my throat.

Standing before me, in her underwear and showing signs of heavy malnutrition and abuse, is Ariel Sharpe. My mother.

She shakes her head slightly, rubbing her eyes. She looks up at me. "Alanna, is it really …?"

I very slowly approach my mother, careful not to startle her. She looks terrible, but at least she's alive. I reach a hand out to hers. "It is, Mom. We're here. You're safe now."

Her eyes glisten. "No we're not, Alanna … we aren't …"

"Mom, Gerard's dead. Dad took care of him."

She looks up at that. "Cole?"

I look to one side and spot the Penitent approaching us, Sabre still tight in his grip. Mom seems afraid of him … memories of the Invader, no doubt … but he finally sheathes his weapon, revealing his smiling self. "It's me, Ariel. The real me." His voice quivers.

Mom's tears are falling fully now. She pulls us both into a three-way embrace, which winds up lowering us down to our knees. The three of us weep for a long time, tears of happiness releasing years of despair at our separation.

It takes all of our combined effort to help Mom back to where we've hidden the van-pack. Before we left, however, Michi and I made sure that the lab would be unusable, using our combined magic and dragon abilities to destroy the hangar. Any remaining dragon embryos left in there will be no further threat. Now we can focus fully on Mom.

Mom slips in and out of consciousness the whole way to the van-pack. My own strength isn't doing too well, either … new clothes notwithstanding, I've had the living crap beaten out of me, so I'm physically in no shape to do any further fighting tonight. Every once in a while, as we carry her, Mom opens up her eyes and looks up at us.

"Just hang in there," Dad tells her. "We're getting you to safety."

She smiles, sighs, and closes her eyes again. I worry every time she does that, worry that she's not going to wake up again.

She opens her eyes and this time looks at me. In her face, despite the darkness, I can see the damage Gerard has done to her with his vile experiments. Her cheeks are sunken, black circles ring her eyes, and her neck looks pencil-thin. I put a hand up to gently stroke her hair. "We're almost there, Mom, take it easy."

She smiles and speaks, and her voice is so weak it makes me want to cry. "I knew you would come for me … both of you …" Her eyes close again. William and Michi share concerned looks with me and Dad, and together we all accelerate. After what seems like an eternity, we arrive at the disembodied van. Dad throws the sliding door open, and the other three of us gently slide Mom into one of the bench seats.

Michi is immediately digging through her own pack, until she finds two half-gallon jugs, filled to the brim with mine and Dad's least-favorite drink. She hands me one bottle. "Dad thought this would come in handy, and I'd be inclined to agree. I can do only so much."

I nod in understanding, climbing into the van next to Mom. Her eyes flutter open again.

"Shhh, don't talk, Mom. Here, drink this." I open the bottle, gently lift her head up, and put the drink to her lips. She sips gently and makes a face.

"At least her tongue still works," Michi remarks, though I'm not so inclined to make jokes at a time like this. Mom takes a couple more sips, and almost immediately it looks like her body's regaining some of its tone.

"That's right, it's medicine, it'll help you." I keep encouraging her to drink more, even though I know I'll probably need some myself for all my injuries. I'd ask Michi to heal me, but she's going to have more pressing healing matters to attend to. I turn back to my best friend. "Are you ready?"

Michi cracks her knuckles. "Let's do this." She trades places with me at Mom's side, laying the gauntleted hand down on Mom's chest. She closes her eyes, casting a silent spell. A bright white glow appears between her fingers and Mom's body, infusing Mom with healing energy.

I slide out of the van-pack, taking a slug of Uncle Cyrus's medical vomit punch as I do, my stomach already threatening to mutiny on the rest of my body by the time I'm at Dad and William's side. Relief colors Dad's face, as well as it must influence mine. I wrap him in my arms. "We found her, Dad."

"We did, Alanna. You figured it out, though. I'm very proud of my little girl."

I smile and hug him tighter. "I couldn't have done it without you."

William sees fit to leave us alone in our daddy-daughter moment, moving into the forest to gather wood for a campfire. The hug seems to last a long time, until we're nearly asleep in each other's arms, until Michi taps me on the shoulder. Even in her new cat form, she looks beat.

"Well, I think I got her stable at least. It's still going to take some time before she's running on all cylinders, but I've been able to reverse some of the damage."

I reach up and squeeze her hand. "Get some rest, girl, looks like you need it."

She nods, and that kitten face of hers grins widely, showing off her sharpened teeth. "I'm getting me some food first. You're welcome to go in and see her."

I look at Dad, who holds up a hand. "You should go first."

I nod and kiss Daddy on the cheek. "I'll be back." I stand up from his lap and walk over to the van-pack, climbing in next to where Mom is lying. Michi's right, she's already looking a lot better, more like the Mom I remember. She opens up her eyes as I enter, and smiles at me.

"Alanna … it's been so long, let me look at you …" I stand next to her, best as I can in the van chassis. Mom's gaze drifts over my entire body. "You've become a beautiful young woman." Her eyes finally lock on my hip, and the Sword that hangs there. Her face takes on a concerned look. "Does this mean …?"

I sigh deeply, holding Mom's hand gently. "Gabe gave it to me the day after you were taken. I told him I wanted to find you, but I got kind of sidetracked and had to find Dad first." I kneel down next to her. "I have to know, Mom, were there any more dragons that we need to take care of?" She squints gently, like she's trying to remember. I don't want to overstress her right now, but if we haven't completely prevented Operation Glass Jaw … whatever it is … then destroying the lab will have been pointless.

"I think there might have been one that was loaned out, but I heard a day or two ago that it had been destroyed." She opens her eyes. "Did you do that?"

I nod. "A lot has changed since you were taken, Mom. I'm sorry."

She reaches up with her free hand and strokes my cheek gently. "It's all right, Alanna. Life is change. It's all we can do as human beings to roll with those changes, and not let them turn us into something we don't want to be."

It's a little too late for that for me, though. I resist saying it, though, but Mom knows it's troubling me.

"Alanna, I'm not quite clear on the rescue, but there was a dragon … a dragon that said it was you."

I bite my lip. *God, I didn't want to have to tell her about this.* "That *was* me, Mom. Gerard got to me about three years ago and injected me with … something … I don't know what it was, but all of a sudden I could do like you do, and grow into a dragon. Even before that, stuff was happening with my body … I found out that I could firecast by accident."

A single tear is rolling down Mom's cheek. "This was never meant to be your burden, Alanna. It was supposed to end with me …"

I bend over and clutch to her shoulders gently. "It's all right, Mom. I've accepted it. I'm not going to let it change who I am. I'm still your little girl. It just so happens that now we're the last dragons."

We hug for a long time, comforting each other, reassuring each other that this moment is real, that these feelings are real. After a long time, I back away when I hear the door open behind me. Dad's standing there.

"That's the other thing, Mom. I found Dad. I brought him back to you."

I slip out of the van, trading places with Daddy. Mom's face lights up. "Cole … it's really you, I've missed you …"

Daddy smiles. "I missed you too, Ari." He leans over and kisses Mom for a long, desperate time, like a drowning man gasping for air. When he lets her lips go, they're both smiling, and Dad puts the icing on the happy cake. "I love you."

I'm watering up. I gently close the sliding door of the van and walk away, until I find William, curled up next to the campfire he's built, a fleece blanket covering his form. Very gently, I slide under the blanket and cuddle up to him, letting emotional sleep overtake me.

Report: Dragon Shot Down at Canadian Border, 2 SSA Pilots Killed in Skirmish

by A. P. Staff

July 15th, 2031

INTERNATIONAL FALLS, MINNESOTA—An unconfirmed report from a Supernatural Security Agency air base near Minneapolis claims that a dragon was intercepted by SSA pilots, who were able to shoot it down despite taking heavy damage to their own aircraft. The pilots were confirmed to have perished in the incident.

The report, acquired for the Associated Press by a knowledgeable source at the base, states that information taken from the aircrafts' video black boxes show the two craft in a dogfight with the dragon, which mysteriously was sporting insignia of the New Empire of America. The report goes on to hypothesize that this may be a misdirection tactic by terror mastermind Alanna Sharpe, to deflect attention from herself and her terrorist network.

When asked about the report at the daily White House briefing, presidential spokesman Ward Gregory dismissed the possibility that the New Empire could be affiliated at all with the dragon. "Utterly preposterous," Mr. Gregory responded. "The Regent Administration has made no uncertain statements on this issue, the supernatural threat is real, it makes regular citizens fearful, and it must be stamped out. To suggest that we would have supernaturals of our own would be hypocritical fantasy. This is clearly a tactic by Sharpe and her supernatural allies, wishing to muddle the sides in this issue."

In her weekly radio address, Vice President Regent also addressed the issue of the markings on the dragon.

"Do not allow yourself to be fooled, my fellow Americans. Alanna Sharpe's terror network is as pernicious as it is deep. She will fool you, then she will turn around and cut your throat when you've come to trust her, much like any supernatural. Their kind has run its course in this world. Those who would rule with fear and unholy power will be flushed from the face of the Earth by the righteous forces of the Supernatural Suppression Agency."

Vice President Regent went on to praise the pilots. "Their noble sacrifice will not be in vain. God bless our fallen heroes, and God Bless Our New Empire."

The pilots' names have not been released to the press, pending the notification of their next of kin.

Chapter Nine: Oval Office

July 17th, continued

I clutch the Sword tightly in my hands, only covered by the Guardswoman's gauntlets. Before me stands Tyrelius Scolar, the giant demonic soul keeping Dad hostage. He raises his sword and taunts me. I grit my teeth, tighten my grip on the Sword, and charge him. He easily ducks my attacks.

I look behind Scolar, to the ice pillar holding Dad's soul captive. Cracks are forming where my tears had fallen on the ice. I get an idea. I reach behind me for the last bottle of holy water.

It's not there.

I frantically search behind me. I hope I just dropped it, that I didn't lose it! Scolar's charging me, I have no time, his blade is driving through my stomach …

I jump awake, eyes wide, breath coming in hard pants, heart hammering in my chest. It takes me a minute to adjust to the feeling of two very strong arms around me. William's, of course, he's cuddling me close to him.

He awakens at about the same time I do. "What's wrong?"

I try to calm my breathing. The campfire has long since gone out, leaving nothing but ashes in its place. I wipe my eyes gently, working all the sleep out of them. "Nothing. It was just a dream … a nightmare, that's all …"

"Do you think they're okay?" William whispers into my ear, looking up toward the van-pack.

"I hope so." I snuggle closer to him, pushing my back into my boyfriend's body. He's real. He feels wonderful, compared to what my brain just subjected me to. "I wouldn't blame them if they both were too tired to do anything this morning."

Suddenly a shriek erupts from the area of the van-pack. Not Mom or Dad, though, it's Michi. "Goddamn, warn a girl why don'tcha?!" She comes jogging over to me, a weird expression on her face that turns apologetic. "God, I'm sorry, Alanna, but I think I just got a good look at your dad's ass."

Oh dear. I cover my face with my embarrassment. Of course, Michi being Michi, she had to announce it as loudly and profanely as possible. William behind me chuckles.

"Oh sure, laugh it up," I playfully tease him. "How would *you* like having your friend walk in on your naked parents?"

He chuckles more. "I'm sorry, when you put it that way …"

I turn around and kiss him, just to let him know I'm not mad. "It's okay. Let's give 'em a couple minutes to get dressed, then see how they're doing."

We both stand up and re-orient ourselves. Most of my injuries from last night seem to have healed. I cautiously try unfurling my wings, and double over in pain: they're completely shredded. I'm not flying *anywhere* anytime soon.

That worries me. I've never been without my wings.

Michi gently takes one of the seriously injured wings in her hands. "I'll work on this when we get a chance, Alanna. In the meantime, keep drinking the potion because every little bit will help."

91

I sigh and nod in resignation. "Okay." Just as I respond and William comes up to my side, the van-pack's side door opens, allowing Mom and Dad to exit.

Dad picked an outfit for Mom out of my pack, and she's adjusting the shirt she's just put on. Even though she's looking better, like her muscle tone is returning, the clothes look deathly loose on her. Dad's still helping her walk, but she's apparently got enough strength to stand on her own feet. I go over to join my family.

"How's she doing?" I ask.

"Better this morning," Dad replies. "Michika and Cyrus do good work."

Mom smiles at me, and I lead her over to my friends. She seems confused as soon as she's in front of Michi. "Kitty? What happened to your human body?"

Michi giggles. "Sorry, Aunt Ariel, it's me."

A glimmer of recognition crosses Mom's face. "Michika? I would never have known, you look so much like your mom did." She accepts a hug from Michi, then turns to face the fourth member of our party. "And who might you be, young man?"

William smiles and extends his hand. "William White Bear, ma'am."

She instantly recognizes the name; that much is clear by her expression and her body language. "Oh, William! From Oklahoma City so long ago, it's so good to see you grown up!"

"It's an honor, ma'am." He gently shakes Mom's hand, as I come back to his side and take his free hand in mine.

Mom's brow rises as she spots our entwined hands. "I had a feeling about this when you two were kids." She grins and hugs me. "You have good taste."

I grin and blush. "So Dad tells me."

Dad clears his throat. "So Alanna, what should we do now?"

That's right, we need a course of action. I'm actually pretty lost, though. Maybe Mom will have an idea … and I think I know where to start. "Come on, Mom, let me get you some breakfast."

Mom smiles at me. "Okay." I take her arm and gently lead her back to the side of the van-pack. Our breakfast this morning apparently consists of a giant pot of oatmeal that Michi cooked. I scoop some into a bowl for Mom, then make one for myself.

Once she starts eating, I sit down next to her. "Mom, what do you know about Operation Glass Jaw?"

She takes a hard swallow. "How did you hear about it?"

"One of the ways we found you was some documentation on Dr. Gerard's experiment, and they mentioned it. What have you heard?"

She takes another swallow. "Before we get into this, I need you to understand one thing. I was basically left helpless in that laboratory, so I got to overhear a lot of things. If I'm going to tell you what I know, you need to understand how I got the information."

I nod and steel myself. "Okay, mom."

She takes my hand gently. "For the last three years, I've been pinned to a wall in a clinical room in the laboratory, wearing nothing but what you found me in, and hooked up to several machines via tubes which were extracting fluids from me." She rolls up the sleeve

93

of her borrowed shirt and allows me to see a double line of pinholes running the length of her green, scaly forearm. "The machines were refining the components of my blood into their respective hormones.

"It was Dr. Gerard's intention to re-start his experiment, but he first had to find out why I was the only survivor. He mixed a cocktail of the chemicals he extracted from me and injected himself with it. It seemed to do nothing to him other than increase his temper. If I tried to talk back at him, it earned me physical abuse. He punched me, kicked me … did things to me." She sighs deeply, but looks up at me again. "About three months in, he got the idea of trying to extract chemicals from other bodily fluids, like sweat, saliva … but he hit his breakthrough …"

She leans against me, and I have no choice but to wrap my arm around her tightly. "It's okay, Mom. Take it slow."

She nods slowly. "He took a sample from my ovaries. With that, he extracted my DNA and injected himself with it. That was the trigger, and it changed him. He had been so frustrated, because I guess in another test subject he'd doubled the dose of the hormones and it had made a dragon …" She sits stock-straight. "Oh my God, that was *you,* wasn't it?"

I nod. "Yeah, he hit me twice, and now I can grow like you." *Now at least I know the source of whatever that stuff was.*

She wipes tears away from her eye. "He extracted more eggs from me, mixed them with his own changed DNA … and he started growing test-tube dragons. This got the attention of the SSA. They came to him, and he showed them around his lab, showed him the first couple of dragons he had bred. They concluded the tour in the room where he was holding me.

"It was three high-ranking blueshirts and the Vice President. She approached me, and I swore her face looked familiar … but I couldn't place it at the moment. She had this weird expression on her face, like she was declaring victory over me. She discussed the situation with Gerard, that she wanted to send a message to the world, and wanted his dragons to do it."

Send a message? Like she did by sending eight dying supernaturals to the Ranch after slicing them up like a sushi chef? My rage quietly builds as Mom continues.

"She mentioned to him that she would want dragons for Operation Glass Jaw, and gave him an order for 25,000 of them, to be fulfilled in two years' time. That was two years ago."

The telling seems to be emotionally exhausting on Mom. She rests her head on my shoulder again. "Whatever it is, Operation Glass Jaw is going to be really bad for the rest of the world, Alanna. I don't know if you were able to stop it by destroying the lab, but you've sure slowed it down somewhat."

I certainly hope so. I clutch Mom's hand. "Thanks, Mom, you've been a great help. You go ahead and get some rest." I pick up her bowl and help her back into the van-pack. Once she's settled in, I turn back to the others, who haven't been able to hide the fact that they've been listening.

Dad is the first to speak. "What do you think?"

I cross my arms and let out a deep breath. "Well, if the Vice President's as cunning as I think she is, there's probably a backup plan for Operation Glass Jaw if her primary plan involving the dragons falls through. We need the details. The only good thing about this situation is that at least we now have a timeline."

"Would the Pentagon have documentation?" Michi asks. "I mean, if it's a defense operation, they should have some sort of word."

Dad shakes his head. "It sounds more like intelligence. If only I still had my CIA contacts …"

"There's another possibility," William chimes in. "What if Operation Glass Jaw was entirely conceived by the President and Vice President?" He turns toward me. "You saw the speech yourself, the Regents are itching to spread their hatred worldwide. What if Operation Glass Jaw is some kind of ruse, to give an excuse for a worldwide war on supernaturals?"

That thought is chillingly logical. It also clinches what we're doing next. Without any preliminary, it comes out of my mouth. "We're going to the White House."

July 18th

Washington, DC is surprisingly quiet for a Friday. Where I was expecting lots of cars on the streets, pedestrians and tourists on the walks, and windows lit up in offices, it's comparatively a ghost town today. Only three or four cars pass by the three of us, not even noticing anything amiss. Every once in a while we cross paths with a pedestrian too busy on his cellphone to notice us.

There's something very wrong with this picture.

Dad offered to stay behind at the van-pack with Mom and help her to recover, while the three of us made our way to the White House. We're about to make the turn onto Pennsylvania Avenue, still closed to traffic as it has been since late 2001, and we still have yet to see more than twenty people out and about at once.

"How are we going to get in once we're there?" William whispers.

"We might have to get creative. Be prepared for action."

Michi cracks her knuckles behind me. "Bring it, Alanna. I'm ready."

Since the integration of all of the armed forces into the SSA, every guard around the White House has been a blueshirt, typically all of them high ranking enlisted men, sergeants and the like. There's three guards standing outside right now, and conveniently enough it's two women and one man. They hold their posts, walking back and forth occasionally, holding rifles on their shoulders.

To our advantage, we have the HoSIPs, and they're going to come in handy for this adventure. I turn back to Michi. "Think you can get us close?"

She smirks. "Watch this!" She jogs over to the guards' position, in front of the male guard. I can't hear the conversation, but it seems to involve a lot of Michi hitching up her skirt in a teasing manner. The next thing we see is all three guards collapsed on the ground. Looking around to make sure no one has seen this, me and William scurry over.

"What did you do?" I ask.

"Oh, just tried to flirt with the one guard, while at the same time casting a sleep spell. They'll be out for the rest of their shift." Michi ransacks the uniform of one of the female guards until she finds a wallet, from which she extracts an SSA ID card, swiping it in her HoSIP. I do the same with the other woman, while William takes the man. When we're finished, and we now look like duplicates of the unconscious guards, we quickly hide the sleeping blueshirts inside their guard booth before walking through the gate and onto the White House grounds.

The inside of the White House is slightly different from all of the photos I've seen, photos of an elegant presidential mansion with reminders of the past residents. Much of the place seems to be in disarray, particularly in the foyer area. Paint and wallpaper is peeling. The paintings of Presidents past have been replaced with giant blow-ups of the Regents' campaign photo-ops.

Good God, how egotistical can you be?

I answer my own question as we continue further into the building. At the foot of the main staircase, flanking it, are two 18-foot marble statues. The Regents, of course, in classical heroic poses; President Carleton Regent stands in a toga, his arm reaching out, orating to the masses, while Vice President Jennifer Regent simply stands in a regal long gown, a crystal tiara upon her head.

William snorts. "They take themselves for gods."

If only you knew what I know …

Michi waves for us to follow her. "This way, guys, the Oval Office is around the corner here." The three of us make our way down the corridor. I'm still a little surprised by how little resistance we've been hitting.

A door that barely appears in the middle of a wall is what greets us. We only can tell it's a door by the knob that's sticking out. My hands shaking, I reach out and grab the knob, turning it slowly. I push the door open.

The stench of death overpowers us immediately. Michi holds her stomach, trying her best not to puke, but William is less successful and runs away to find a bathroom. I continue pressing forward … the smell of death is nothing compared to the Inferno, after all. I open the door fully and walk into a completely dark room. The curtains are drawn, all the lights are off … even a computer I can kind of see in a corner is powered down. Dust is coating many of the surfaces of the office, in some places looking nearly inches thick. Cobwebs spread from one end to the other. It looks like a bad Halloween haunted house to my eye.

Michi, coughing and breathing through her mouth, catches up to me. "What the hell?"

That's what I'm afraid of.

I make my way across the office, to where I know there's a window, by the President's desk. I search in the gloom for a break in the curtain, only realizing once I'm up close that these curtains are black. I clutch the curtains and swing them wide open, bathing the office in light.

Michi shrieks in surprise. When I turn around to ask her what's wrong, I instantly see it. There's a very dead body, sitting in the chair behind the desk, face-down and sprawled across the desk. Across the back of the body's neck is a half-moon shaped incision, opening widely and exposing the interior of the corpse's neck.

It's all I can do to keep my lunch down at this sight. With trembling fingers, I reach under the head and lift it up to see the face.

No. It can't be …

It's President Regent.

"Hey! What are you doing?"

The shout of an older man takes me away from the corpse. I look up and see a bureaucrat standing in the doorway, cellphone in hand, reaching into his coat for what looks like a pistol.

Damn. So this is how we're going to die.

Chapter Ten: Operation Glass Jaw

July 18th, continued

Michi leaps into action, grabbing the bureaucrat by the neck and flinging him on the couch of the office. A huge cloud of dust billows from the furniture, in the midst of which Michi drops her camouflage body and wraps her gauntleted hand around the suit's throat. A cat snarl comes from their general area. I drop the President's head back down to the desk and join the two of them in the middle of the room. William rushes in at this point and closes the door.

"What happened?" He wipes his mouth. *Poor guy …*

"Oh, not much, Willie," Michi chimes up through gritted teeth, "just doing some late spring cleaning, getting rid of dead bodies and the contents of this asshole's bowels." She narrows her eyes at the bureaucrat. "Hang up your phone, or you're gonna need a cork to drink your next cup of coffee." She tightens her grip on his neck for emphasis.

The suit is clearly fearful. He looks like he's about to cry. He drops the phone, bringing his other hand out of his coat.

Maybe it's time to take advantage of my reputation, undeserved as it is. I step to the side of Michi and power down my HoSIP. Our new captive's eyes widen once he sees me.

"I assume you know who I am, right?"

He nods. Right now he can't speak, since Michi has a death grip on his voicebox.

"Okay. My associate here is going to let you have your neck back, and we're going to have a nice conversation. I can guarantee you, though, that if you try to run, or tell anyone we were here, that we will find you and kill you. Are we in agreement?"

He nods fearfully. I think right now he'd agree to hang from the ceiling from his toes if it meant we'd keep him alive.

"Okay then. Michi, if you please." She releases the bureaucrat's throat, pulling him up to a seated position on the dusty couch. I stand over him, my arms crossed. I let smoke trickle slightly out of my nose, just to show him I mean business. "All right, let's start with the basics. What's your name?"

His voice sounds almost squeaky and quivering, but he manages to speak. "I'm Ward … Ward Gregory, the White House spokesman."

I've heard of this guy … the mouthpiece of the Administration. "Good, we're getting somewhere. All right. When was the last time you came into this office?"

He looks at me fearfully, then back at the desk with the cadaver on it. "I've never been in here."

My hand reaches my chin. "Are you sure?"

"Positive, ma'am."

I motion to Michi. She sits down next to Gregory, placing the gauntleted hand on the side of his head. He tenses up slightly, then relaxes as she doesn't clench her fingers but instead casts a spell, making his face glow orange.

"He's telling the truth, Alanna. He's worked here for nine years and never came in here once."

At least I know he's truthful now. "So be it. If you never came in here, how did you issue statements from the President?"

He sighs deeply. "They were prepared long before I would give my briefings by staffers. Sometimes I'd get them directly from the Vice President herself."

William in the meantime has walked over to the desk and is inspecting the body, looking almost like a coroner. I keep him in the corner of my vision while interrogating Gregory. "What do you know about Operation Glass Jaw?"

He swallows hard. "Glass Jaw? But … but I haven't said anything about …"

"I have my sources," I interrupt. He doesn't need to know my sources are Mom and Scol … Dad. "Just tell me. What is Operation Glass Jaw?"

He loosens his tie. Clearly he's nervous about it.

"Did I say something to make you more nervous, Mr. Gregory?"

He nods his head. "Operation Glass Jaw … it's Vice President Regent's idea, honest, not mine, not anyone else's …"

I crouch down to his level. "You can tell me, Ward." I put a hand gently on his shoulder. "I'm not the monster that Mrs. Regent would make me out to be. I just want to know what Glass Jaw is. What's the target? What's the scope?"

He fidgets with his fingers for a long time before looking up at me. "Operation Glass Jaw is a concentrated attack on every world capital. We have a standing order … at the military labs at Pax River … for a large number of dragons, which are to be programmed to cause general chaos worldwide."

I'm getting angrier with every word. "What's the purpose?"

"To convince the United Nations that supernaturals are a threat on a global scale. And to gain authorization to spread the SSA around the world from the body."

Damn it. "How was it going to be justified?"

His voice shakes. "W ... we were ... we're going to blame you." He looks up at me. "God, you're no older than my own daughter ..."

"Save it, pal. I don't particularly like being framed or manipulated." I growl softly and go back over to the desk, standing by William. Michi raises her hand again to Gregory's head.

William is almost too closely examining the wound on Carleton Regent's corpse. His eyes seem very confused. I crouch down next to him. "What's wrong?"

"This doesn't make a damn bit of sense at all." He points a finger at parts of the wound. "See this? It's blood."

It looks more like brown mud and water to me. "Are you sure?"

"Positive. This wound ... it's fresh, but it's like a wound that's made during an autopsy. It didn't create fresh blood." He points to the water. "His blood's separated into its component parts." He points at other places in the wound. "These also look very atrophied and decayed, like they haven't really been used for a long time."

I don't want to ask, but I do anyway. "How long?"

He shrugs and stands upright. "I'd guess ... years, probably."

"Wait, wait," I exclaim. "Are you telling me the President of the New Empire is a *zombie?*"

"Was, at least. There isn't a spark of life left to him. I don't think the spark of life's been here for a long, long time." William leads me away from the corpse, back over to the couch with Michi and Gregory.

The aide looks up at us. "What are you going to do with me? Kill me?"

My, what effective propaganda you have. "It's not worth my time to kill you, Mr. Gregory. You're coming with us. We need as much detail about Glass Jaw as possible, and you're going to be our ticket to getting it."

Michi picks up Gregory by his arm and leads him toward the door. "Where are we going?" he whimpers.

"To the East Wing. You said it yourself, Vice President Regent was the one behind Glass Jaw. We're going to the First Lady's office."

William places a blanket over the dead body and follows us out of the Oval Office. By this time, several other SSA guards of the place have been alerted to our presence … no doubt our unlucky victims outside have come to and sounded some kind of alarm. Michi's already fighting off a couple of them, but I figure that there's a more effective means of backing them off. I rush up and wrap my arm around Gregory's neck, blowing smoke out of my nose.

"Back off! We have the White House spokesman, if you want him to live lay down your weapons!"

A couple of the agents do as we demand. One at the front, though, a young lieutenant, sneers at us. "Do your worst, Sharpe. We can always find another spokesman."

Gregory whimpers more in my grip. I don't blame him.

105

"Fine, you asked for it. Michi?"

Michi raises her arm toward the group of attackers. *"SUSPENSION!"*

The entire group, numbering 15 or so, is forcefully yanked up by their hands and feet toward the ceiling, the after effect of the spell being a cluster of human chandeliers. Hopefully this spell last as long as we need to get the information. We rush across the main room, past the statues and the staircase, and into the East Wing. It's not long until we find the office we're searching for.

I was prepared for a lot of things, but not this. When we open the door of the office, the entire place is wall-to-wall newspaper clippings, photographs, and scrawled drawings. It looks more like a psycho killer's bedroom than the office of the Vice President. Buried under a large quantity of detritus is the desk, next to a window painted black. I almost don't want to enter out of fear for my health, but the answers we need are in here.

I push Gregory through the door. "In you go, Ward. Help us out."

He staggers through the mess, and I follow him in. Michi and William are close behind, and are equally as distracted by the displays on the walls as I am. I take a closer look at some of the junk.

Newspaper clippings from 2011, yellowed and crumbling, discuss strange events taking place around the world. A report from Scotland about Loch Lomond turning blood red. The irradiating of St. Louis due to a fallen satellite. Mysterious weather patterns appearing around Four Corners.

I shiver. *Four Corners … Abaster. She's been obsessing about Four Corners now for two* decades!

My eyes shift slightly rightward, to some of the scrawled drawings. Crudely-shaped human forms are engraved rather than sketched into paper, so deeply that occasionally holes appear within lines. Two figures have swords, fighting each other on one page. On another page, a giant human figure with a sword and wings fights another giant figure. On a third page, there's a cartoonish dragon looking out and taunting the viewer.

I realize that I'm hyperventilating slightly. I turn around to the desk. Gregory is digging through stacks of paper, then slows up and produces a single file folder. "Here it is."

We all rush over to where Gregory holds the documentation, and I take the folder from him. In broad, black letters, the title is stamped into the file.

OPERATION GLASS JAW
HIGHEST CLEARANCE
EYES ONLY

"Screw clearance," Michi offers. "Open it up."

I nod at this suggestion and open the file, looking through the papers. As I continue to read, my eyes widen, to the point that they must take up half of my head by the time I'm finished, because William is shaking my shoulder.

"Alanna, what is it?"

I slam the folder shut. "We need to take this. We don't have a lot of time." I turn to Gregory. "Thank you for your assistance, Mr. Gregory. We won't take up any more of your time."

He loosens his tie and unbuttons his collar. "If it's all the same to you, I think I'd rather come with you."

I raise an eyebrow. "Why is that?"

"If I'm *that* disposable, why should I stay here? You heard those guards, they didn't care if you killed me or not. To hell with this job, I'm leaving and coming with you."

It takes me a moment to take in that this is probably the quickest onset of Stockholm syndrome in the history of mankind, but only a moment. "Okay then. Let's go, guys." I clutch the folder tightly and lead the group out of the office.

Unfortunately, we're met by another company of SSA troops, this one double the size of the previous company. They already have guns blazing at us, which isn't helping our situation any.

I toss the file folder over to Michi. "Keep this safe. William, with me!" I draw the Sword and rush toward the troopers, while William releases the wendigo. We run, heads down, into the midst of their numbers before starting our side of the fight. The Sword knocks aside many of the troops, careful as I am not to point the edge toward any of them; even if they're with the enemy, they're still only the pawns of the real evil. The wendigo, though, isn't quite as discriminating.

The beast must be hungry …

Screams echo through the chamber as the wendigo tears into troopers left and right. I'm suddenly stopped in mid-swing … *screaming … terrible, nonstop screaming from all corners, like in Hell. Damned souls reaching out to*

108

me, trying to steal my Sword, steal my life … take my life and virtue. Falling into the river Styx …

The Guardswoman starts hyperventilating. I drop to my knees, putting my hands up to my ears, rocking. The Sword drops out of my hand, shrinking me back down into myself. I'm screaming now. "Make it stop! Make it stop! *MAKE IT STOP!*"

The last dragon's roar is accompanied by a wide fire stream, blasting away at most of the remaining troopers, forcing them through the foyer and blowing a wide hole in the front façade of the White House. I didn't mean to blast them. It just happened.

I'm shaking, and I'm collapsing, and I'm shutting down … why is this happening? What is happening to me? I'm frightened … the wendigo is coming over to me …

Don't let him eat me! He's going to consume me! Get him away from me!

I shriek and start scurrying away from the monster, even as he starts shrinking back into William, who's looking incredibly hurt. My heart is racing. I almost can't tell where we are anymore.

William continues to approach, but instead of consuming me he picks me up in his strong arms. I'm still shuddering. Michi, meanwhile, has been levitating the Sword and slips it back into its scabbard. I'm panting still. I look up at William.

His face shows his concern. "Are you okay?"

I can't talk, all I can do is pant, and shake my head. I clutch his shirt and pull myself tightly to him. He carries me as all of us leave the White House.

Chapter Eleven: The Final Gambit

July 19th

I awaken in my bed at the Ranch. I have no idea how I got here, but I do know that I'm comfortable and I don't want to leave. I'm also aware of another person in the room with me. Two people, actually. I sit up in the bed. "Mom? Dad?"

"We're here, Alanna," Mom intones. She comes over to the bed and sits down. She's looking much better now than she had been, but still not quite to the shape I remember her being in. There's still some long-term effects of being held that she's feeling, I'm certain. "You had a rough day yesterday."

I rub my eyes. "How did I get back here anyway? Did we fly again?"

Dad shakes his head. "Apparently there was some kind of device that Gabe and Cyrus built into the van that sent us straight back to the Ranch."

My mind drifts to that mysterious teleporting pen that Gabe always seems to have on him, that takes us right here. I smile slightly. *He gave it to us.*

"Alanna, William told us what happened in the White House. Do you want to tell us anything?" Mom strokes my cheek gently.

I sigh deeply. "I don't know what it was. One minute I was fighting the blueshirts, and then the next I was a panicking ball of fear, because they wouldn't stop screaming …"

The screams are coming back in my mind. I clutch my ears and curl up in a tight ball, trying to make them go away. I'm barely aware of Dad coming to the bed, sitting with me.

"I need to make the screams stop, I keep hearing them …"

He puts a hand on my knee gently. "I know. They seem like they won't go away, don't they?"

My breathing is speeding up. "Yeah. I hear them in my dreams, I hear them all day, I hear them echoing in every corner of my brain."

Mom sits on the other side of me from where Dad is sitting, wrapping her arms around me. "Your father told me about the things you did to find him, Alanna."

I look up at Mom. "The whole story?"

She smiles gently. "All I really needed to know. You don't have to ever think about that place again, it's over, it's done. You brought your father back. He's with us now, he's holding us, loving us again."

My breathing starts to slow and lengthen. I look over at Mom. "I did things there. Things I'm not proud of. I fought people. I tormented souls. I tried to kill my guide once, even though he was already dead." I look over at Daddy. "I destroyed a Sharpe, Dad, I didn't tell you that."

He pulls his hand back gently. "What do you mean?"

I stand up. "Exactly what it sounds like. I ran into a bunch of our ancestors, hellbound Sharpes, every single one angling to take the Sword back. One of them tried to grab it, and instead of pulling it out of the scabbard the hilt of it destroyed him just because of how long he held it." My hands are on my head. "I'm sorry, I really am … I can't take this." I rush out of the room.

111

It's not them, that's for sure. It's not my parents that are the cause for this stress. It wasn't even the White House invasion, either ... although they started there, I don't think our fight there was the reason for these flashbacks. I find that I can only run for a short time before my heart races uncontrollably. I lean against a wall clutching my chest, panting and heaving.

Someone's coming ... they can't see me like this, but at the same time I feel so weak right now. I dully look up toward the approaching figure, and feel somewhat relieved when the shadow is revealed to belong to Julian.

"Alanna? Are you okay?" He rushes to my side and brushes my hair away from my face.

"I think so," I weakly respond. He takes my hand and leads me down the hallway. "Where have you been? I haven't seen you in a while."

Julian chuckles. "I was just settling in Mr. Gregory. He's going to have a lot of culture shock around here, much like I did." He leads me over to the table. "Right now I'm worried about you."

I'm shaking, I suddenly realize. I try to slow down my breathing. "It's okay, Julian, really. I'm just a little tired, I think." I look over toward the kitchen. "I'll just get some food ..."

"Alanna, I know what's going on here."

Julian's frank assertion catches me short. "What do you mean?"

He pats my shoulder. "I've worked with enough vets to know PTSD when I see it. A couple guys I used to work with at the phone company were war vets, and every once in a while they'd have flashbacks. I dealt with a really bad one once, and he looked just like you

112

do … couldn't catch his breath, shaking, looking like he was going to panic and run away at any moment."

Now that he mentions it, I do feel a little bit like an extremely nervous bird. I sigh deeply.

"Want to talk about it? I helped the other guys before, but I had to get them really drunk to do it."

I look up at Julian, sighing. "I don't think you can help with the flashbacks, but … I can tell you, they started when I read the file we brought back."

He nods, stroking his chin. "The battle plan, you mean?"

"Right, that one. It's … I don't know, it's just disturbing, what's in the plan. I wanted to run away from it the instant I picked it up … honestly I wanted to go somewhere else the instant we went into the Vice President's office."

Julian puts a hand on my shoulder. "It's okay to be afraid, Alanna. Fear is part of what makes us human, after all. It's just how you deal with that fear that determines what *kind* of human."

I sigh deeply. "How do I deal with this?"

He shrugs. "A few ways. Some people just simply run away. They try to keep themselves out of danger, try to keep their sanity, and stay out of the way. A few people stick with whatever they're doing despite the fear, but let the fear consume them so that they always live in fear. For them, fear becomes a way of life, and they forget how to live without it.

"The truly rare people in this world, though, stand up to their fears, face them down, and don't flinch. These are the heroes. And I believe in you, Alanna, I believe that you are a hero. You can stand up to this fear."

113

I look up and smile at the older man. *His face ... now that I have fresh memories, I can see the resemblance ...*

"Alanna?"

Mom's voice interrupts the moment. She and Dad are coming out of the hallway and into the dining room. When Julian looks over, I see the shock cross his expression.

"Alanna, are you okay?" Mom approaches us.

"I'm better," I respond, as I stand up from the table. "There's someone here I think you want to meet." I nudge Julian to a standing position, in front of Mom. Now that they're together, I see Mom is about a head taller than Julian, but their faces confirm they're family.

Julian's really nervous, but he tries to hide it. I'm watching his chest expand and retract quickly as he tries to compose the right words in his mind. Finally he reaches his hand out to Mom.

"Are you Ariel?"

Mom nods, looking a little confused, not that I can blame her for that. "I am. And you would be?"

Julian smiles. "Someone who's wanted to meet you for a long time. My name is Julian. Julian Vibria."

The shock is obvious on Mom's face. She's the one that needs a seat ... she could be knocked over with a shallow breath. Julian sits down with her.

"Ariel, I'm your father."

Dad comes over to my side and puts an arm around my shoulders, leading me away. For sure there's a lot of questions they're going to be asking each other, and we both know that it's not our place to eavesdrop. Our path winds up taking us into the living room area, where Dad lets me go so I can rejoin William at his side.

He seems a little resistant. "Are you all right?" I ask him.

"Ask me later," he responds, and that's all.

Michi and Gabe are sitting at the table by the fireplace. On the table is the cause of all of my trouble, the Operation Glass Jaw mission profile. Gabe looks up at me.

"Okay, so you found this file. Alanna, you're the only one who's read this yet. Would you mind filling all of us in on the details?"

Do I have to?

Aunt Kitty and Uncle Cyrus enter and take their own seats at the table. I take a deep breath and reach for the file, opening it up.

"Okay … so Dad's breadcrumb that led to Mom involved the military lab and the order of 25,000 dragons for Operation Glass Jaw. The intended use for those dragons was to cause worldwide panic and mayhem by attacking every UN capital simultaneously. According to the plan, this would create conditions that would activate the President's war powers, and allow for the spread of the SSA around the globe. They have a backup plan in case the dragons aren't ready.

"That backup plan involves demons. A number of lesser demons are also positioned in all of those cities, awaiting a signal to attack. Regardless of who the attackers are, the mission profile shows that SSA deep cover agents in each city would defeat the 'aggressors,' using standard SSA strategies and equipment. So basically, it's a grand con game."

115

Gabe strokes his chin. "I see. I think we can organize a counterattack to the operation in enough time to prevent it."

"That's only Phase One, though."

Now I have everyone's undivided attention. I flip two pages into the file … to the part that started all the trouble. I take a deep, shaky breath.

"Phase Two takes place on home soil. According to this, the SSA has been spending massive amounts of time and money analyzing the movements …" I'm shaking, but I need to get this out. "… analyzing the movements of the Hidden-In-Plain-Sight Ranch."

A collective gasp comes from the group. "They're hunting us?" Aunt Kitty asks.

"Apparently so. Phase Two is designated to take place at the same time as the global attacks. The plan according to this is to assemble all 20 SSA troops in the continental New Empire at a forecast location where they project the Ranch will appear in three months. When the Ranch appears, the attack will begin." I flip a page in the file. "During this battle, Phase Three will occur. Phase Three is also referred to in the documentation as the 'final gambit.'"

A sense of dark dread hovers over all of us. I'm sure all of them don't want to know what the final gambit is, but they need the information. Gabe looks almost ashen as he speaks. "So then, what is Phase Three?"

I swallow hard. "Phase Three involves a single high-level party of SSA agents accompanying a new commander into the Ranch, where that commander will find the Avalon door." My body's broken out in a cold sweat. This is so much harder than it seems like it would be. "The commander will cross through the

Avalon door and plunge the Damnation Blade into Avalon's soil."

Uncle Cyrus goes even paler than usual. Gabe groans. "Of course, I should have seen this coming."

Dad looks agitated. "What is it, Gabe? I think the time for half-statements is over."

I feel William's arm wrapping around my shoulders as Gabe begins his explanation. "I think we talked about this before, the Damnation Blade can kill gods. It's the power of disbelief; once it wounds something with a large amount of belief behind it, disbelief takes over, and the injured party succumbs from this. If someone were to take the Damnation Blade to Avalon and … well, literally *stab* Avalon with it, then this disbelief will cause the destruction of Avalon."

Aunt Kitty narrows her eyes. "The stakes are really high, aren't they?"

"Even higher than you know. If Avalon dies, every supernatural being who draws their power from an Avalonian source also dies."

Aunt Kitty and Michi immediately clutch Uncle Cyrus. My thoughts immediately drift to the Lady in the Lake … I'm so fearful for her now.

"Just the Avalonians?" William asks.

"Not just them, not by a longshot. *Every single supernatural on Earth* derives their power from some aspect of Avalon." Gabe stands up and grabs the file. "This final gambit of theirs is an extermination ploy."

New Empire President Found Dead: Alanna Sharpe Responsible

By A. P. Staff
July 19th, 2031

WASHINGTON—Sources from the White House confirm that beloved New Empire President Carleton Regent, whose popularity and legend are unmatched in American history, was found dead from a supernatural-inflicted wound at his desk in the Oval Office. The Supernatural Suppression Agency immediately released a revised warrant on notorious terror mastermind Alanna Sharpe, adding the assassination of the president to her list of crimes.

Sharpe and her associates conducted a terrorist operation at the White House, a skirmish which left several SSA agents injured and a large part of the White House destroyed. Currently missing after the conflict is White House spokesman Ward Gregory, presumed being held hostage by Sharpe's supernatural forces.

President Regent's death, by the Constitution, elevates his wife and Vice President Jennifer Regent to the office of the President. In a written statement released by Mrs. Regent's office, the new President affirmed that Sharpe would meet justice. "I have just taken the Oath of Office, and will be taking time to mourn the loss of not only my husband but a great man who led the New Empire to higher reaches. In the meantime, Alanna Sharpe should be advised that assassinating Carleton amounts to an act of war, and as such will trigger the war powers clause Congress granted in one of my husband's last acts on this

118

Earth. The supernatural threat is in its death throes after this incident. God bless Carleton Regent, and God Bless Our New Empire."

Dead Calm

Chapter Twelve: The Muster

July 20th

The sun rises on what may be one of my last mornings on this planet. The knowledge of this gets heavier with each passing moment as I awaken and sit up in bed, my eyes traveling up to the mountain lion head.

I pat my old, taxidermied friend on his wrinkled snout, in mid-snarl. "I never thought you would outlast me."

The dead glass eyes in the trophy stare back, impassive, much like I need to be this morning. After all, today I start mustering our troops.

At the conclusion of the meeting when I revealed the battle plan for Operation Glass Jaw, we formalized our initial loose plan to train the supernaturals we have rescued to fight. Every one of us is scheduled to conduct one day of training a week each for the next month, to prepare our forces for the eventual siege on the Ranch.

Each of us drew straws for which day we would lead the training. Teresa Iles drew Mondays, to train on physical aptitudes, like running, jumping, and evading fire. Michi drew Tuesdays, where she's taking the magic users through their ropes, while the non-magic supernaturals continue physical training. Wednesdays fell to Aunt Kitty, who's taken it upon herself to teach all of us how to fire every weapon she has available at the Ranch. William drew Thursdays, when he's teaching field triage and first aid. Fridays were drawn by Gabe, who uses it as a strategy day, to share New Empire tactical data and countermeasures. Uncle Cyrus got Saturdays, which he's using to train the last-line defenders how to fully guard the Avalon door, while all the others continue training on their own.

I wound up with Sundays. Which meant I wound up first. I haven't the damnedest idea what I'm going to do with these people, but I'll give it my best shot. I dress in clothes suitable for light physical activity and head down to the dining room. Aunt Kitty stands by the counter, serving up plates of food to us all.

She gives me my plate. "Don't get too nervous today, kiddo. They need you on top of your game."

I smirk. "Thanks." The added pressure isn't helping me one bit. Michi waves frantically over to me, and I join her quickly at the table. William, oddly, is kind of distant … he's talking with Dad fairly animatedly, but I don't know why.

Michi quickly pulls my attention away from them. "So what are you going to train us in today?"

I give a non-committed shrug. "I don't really know, actually. Everybody else has certain specialties. All I have is accidental heroism under my belt."

Michi punches me playfully, but with her new supernatural strength it hurts like hell. "Don't worry, Alanna. You're going to be fine. After all, accidental heroism is something that's in short supply, so we need a little bit more."

I give a sly wink to my best friend. "I'm sure." I look back over toward William and Dad. Every so often William looks up at me, barely acknowledging my presence, but then he turns back to Dad and rejoins their conversation. I sigh deeply, picking at my breakfast.

"What happened between you two?" Michi ponders. "Did you guys have a fight?"

"What? No, no we didn't," I retort with a start. "It's just … well, since we got back from DC, he's been so … solitary on me. I think I accidentally insulted him or something … he won't come close to me, and he certainly doesn't give as much affection as he did before."

Michi looks back over to where William and Dad are talking, then back at me. "Ahh, don't worry about it. I think if you give him a few days, things'll be right back to where they were. Besides, even if I'm wrong, you still got me." She winks and holds out her pinky. "BFF's to the end, right?"

I can't help but laugh, as I loop my own pinky with hers. "BFF's to the end." The seriousness of the situation is starting to sink in on me, and I suddenly grasp Michi's entire hand. "Sisters beyond the end."

Michi seems startled for a moment, then gives a warm smile. "Sisters." She clutches my hand tightly once more before standing up and leaving the table. I turn my attention back to the scrambled eggs and chopped bison steak on the plate in front of me, my appetite newly returned. All through breakfast, though, I keep an eye on William and Dad.

With food down me, I head outside to the main field of the Ranch, to where Uncle Cyrus and Gabe are already standing. With them is a large crowd of supernaturals, roughly about two hundred in number, all of them looking as confused as I feel. Gabe motions for me to join him, and I pick up my pace to meet the two men.

"How do things look this morning?" I ask gently.

"Fair to middling," Uncle Cyrus responds. "This is all the supernaturals we could muster together from our rescues, all of them have been brought back from Avalon, and all of them are really reluctant to fight."

Gabe's eyes darken. "It's going to be up to you to show them that they can survive battle, and that they can win this war. You'll have to be an example."

Always the icon. Of course.

"I'll do my best," I respond, "although this group looks pretty rough."

"They'll get the polish from the other instructors," Gabe insists. "What they need from you is training on how to be a supernatural."

"Many of these people only have latent powers, which means they haven't really used their powers extensively yet," Uncle Cyrus explains. "A lot of them are self-conscious about them, life in the New Empire doing that to a person with powers."

I can certainly understand that. Even the *suspicion* you might be a supernatural tends to get you scurried off to a far-away prison cell in the New Empire, so for sure these actual supernaturals won't want to be showing off.

"Are you ready?" Gabe asks.

I close my eyes, trying to find a place of inner peace. My mind laughs at me. "As ready as I'll ever be."

"Your audience awaits, then." Gabe motions to the front of the group, where he has a bullhorn waiting.

I walk over to the tool and pick it up, flipping on its switch and speaking into it. "May I have your attention, please?" My voice booms over the heads of the group, who stop their individual conversations to turn their attention my way. "Thank you. If you don't know me, I should introduce myself. My name is Alanna Sharpe, and I will be training you today."

"You? Train us?" One voice cracks wise at the back of the group. "You're a kid yourself!"

The crowd parts so that I can see my opposition. It's an older man, looking around forty or so, and his eyes are glowing. I start walking toward him. "What's your name, sir?"

He smirks and crosses his arms. "It's Urich. Samuel Urich."

"Well, Mr. Urich, what are your supernatural abilities?"

"Uh, hell-LO!" He points at his eyes. "These glowy eyes got my ass in trouble from every SSA troop from here to Bakersfield. What do you think?"

I'm now face-to-face with him. Sort of ... he's about five inches taller. "And what use are those 'glowy eyes' of yours in a fight? Do you even know how to use them to your advantage?"

I might have caught him off balance, but he's not showing it. "Sure I do. I stare, someone else shoots. I try not to die."

"A little too simplistic," I retort. "There's got to be some reason why your eyes glow." My rage is starting to climb the longer this conversation continues.

Urich snorts. "You're supposed to be that super-scary terrorist? What's *your* supernatural power, texting your boyfriend 24 hours a day?"

I narrow my eyes. "Have you fought the SSA?"

"Yeah, why do you think I'm here?"

127

"Have you had to fight them every single day for years? Have you had your entire family taken away from them? Have you had the SSA target you specifically as a wanted criminal so that no place in the nation was safe for you? *That's my life* right now, Mr. Urich."

Urich snorts again. *He sounds like a pig ...* "And what about that makes you qualified to teach us *anything,* little girl?"

That tears it. Images start echoing through my mind, specifically Scolar's insistence on calling me "hatchling." The rage bubbles over, as does the burning coming up my throat. I launch a fire stream right into Urich's midsection, blasting him backward and over a large group of the other supernaturals behind him, who all rush to his side once he lands to put out his flaming clothes.

I let out a long puff of smoke from my nose. "Does anyone else have an objection?" I scream at the rest of the assemblage. Quiet murmuring is all I get in response. "All right then. I'm tasked with training all of you in how to use your supernatural abilities to your advantage in battle. This is something you will need to know if you are to survive the coming fight. The SSA will no longer take prisoners, this is now a fight for our very survival."

More murmuring, this time of the worried variety. Samuel Urich finally stands up again and is helped back over to the group, but this time he remains quiet.

"For the next month of Sundays, I will be helping all of you get a handle on your supernatural abilities. We will explore every aspect of your powers, leave no stone unturned. You will know everything there is to know about yourself by the time we're finished with this, and every possible way you can use those powers. Even the most seemingly useless power will be useful."

The rest of the group sits down on the ground, listening intently to me. I'm not used to this kind of attention … I'm not entirely sure I like it. One man raises his hand, and thankfully it's someone I recognize, Jerry Tile. "How will you be dividing us up?"

"Good question, thank you. You will be divided into two divisions, Attack and Support. Those of you with powers that create chaos and destruction … powers like the one I just used … you will be in the Attack division. Anyone whose power can be weaponized will basically be in this division. The rest of you, those who have powers more aimed toward recovery and healing, will be in the Support division. Jerry, for instance, your power to rebuild weapons and equipment puts you in the Support division."

Jerry nods in confirmation.

"Everyone, today will be the day that we make the divisions. You will need to demonstrate your supernatural abilities before myself, Mr. Salem, and Mr. Francis." I motion toward Uncle Cyrus and Gabe. "We will be making the decisions on who goes into which division. For now, please form an orderly line, and we will take you in turn to a secluded field for your demonstrations."

The rest of the day is spent evaluating powers, and taking notes on who's available and who is the most powerful. Jerry, naturally, winds up in the Support division. Because he isn't training, Trent Gracin gives us a demonstration of exactly what his insect powers

129

entail, which earns him a spot in the Attack division. Samuel Urich, it turns out, is a healer and those "glowy" eyes produce x-rays; while it's all the more reason for me to blast him above and beyond his insubordination, he winds up in the Support division as a medic, and I give him precise instructions to get additional medical training from William and Grandmother.

Some of these supernaturals will be more useful than others. One of them has a power almost identical to Yolanda French's, only instead of producing projectile guns from their arms they spew various forms of caustic gas; definitely the Attack division. Many of the Attack division supernaturals have obvious gifts which will help in a fight, but others are more subtle such as Lydia Dales, a woman I met at my birthday party three years ago whose power involved producing wine from her hands. Isaac Portland, the explosive flatulence supernatural from the same party, also winds up in Attack.

The Support division is less than half the Attack division by the end of the day, however, and includes many folks who came to the Ranch while I was in the Inferno. Betty Rancin, a mechanic who apparently can repair any intricate machine she touches through a psychic ability, naturally gets a Support role. So do Tyler Wauk, whose ability involves sucking poisons out of other people, and Quincy Alenia, whose ears can tune into any radio frequency; Quincy in particular will be useful for picking up reports of enemy movements. By the time the sun sets, we have our exact numbers for each division. Both Uncle Cyrus and

Gabe count up and confirm their numbers before handing me a tally sheet.

SUPPORT: 38 Healers, 18 Communicators, 24 Fix-Its, 80 total

ATTACK: 83 Projectile, 58 Close Quarters, 66 Mages, 19 Defensive, 226 total

TOTAL FORCES: 306

It looks like a register for Dungeons and Dragons. If only it wasn't the entire force defending supernaturals everywhere from an enormous enemy army looking to eliminate them all from the face of the planet.

Chapter Thirteen: Lunge for Bliss

July 20th, continued

Dinner's calling, and my stomach is growling, but I'm almost too stressed to eat. Shooting Urich didn't help my stress level much, and it certainly isn't helping my mood. I take a plate of food, but I'm simply picking at it. There's so much on my mind tonight. The fight's coming up, and I have such a small force. Everyone's so focused on their individual tasks, there's no time for friendship, for laughter, for camaraderie anymore. Even William's backed off of me.

I start shaking. I try to take bites of food to calm myself, but it's not working. I look up at the activity around me. Michi and her parents are eating together tonight … and I think Aunt Kitty and Uncle Cyrus are holding hands for the first time I've ever seen. Mom and Dad are with them as well, chatting and catching up.

It's kind of nice to think of the four of them, trading war stories, reunited once more. When they were in the military, on their team, they did mighty things. They defeated many demons around the world, defended life, made the world safer for humanity and supernaturals alike. They stopped the end of the world once, while Mom was carrying me. I only hope that the force we're building now can live up to that level of greatness.

I hope we can preserve life like they did, long ago.

I try to take another bite, but darkness is starting to overcome me. I look back over at my parents, and Aunt Kitty and Uncle Cyrus …

The nightmare comes back, the nightmare from Hell. Uncle Cyrus and Aunt Kitty berate me, wasting their help. Mom and Dad, never together again, are tortured and raped. The souls in the Styx grasp at me, pulling me further down into the bottomless waters. The centaurs have me at their mercy, straddling me one at a time …

"Alanna? Are you okay?"

A light touch on my shoulder startles me. My adrenaline is going too strongly, and I instantly stand up from the table and back away from the person who just came up to me.

It's William. He looks bewildered. "Alanna, it's just me, it's all right." He raises his hands, palms toward me.

My mind puts William into the worst situation … *another Hell nightmare where he ate me and went with Michi instead …* I turn around and run away in a panic. My running doesn't end until I reach the safety of my room, the darkness surrounding me. I close the door and collapse down on the floor.

Insistent knocking. "Alanna? Please open up, it's just me."

William again. I'm still in shock, still shaking. "Please go away, I don't …"

"I can't go away, not yet. There's something going on, Alanna. Please let me in." His voice sounds like it's failing at the last words.

I reach up and turn the knob. A shaft of light enters the room, followed by the figure of William, who crouches down next to me on the floor. "Alanna, what's going on?"

I curl my legs up into my arms tightly, burying my face in my knees. "God, I don't know … I just want it all to stop, to go away …"

He slides up next to me. "Alanna, if you need to talk, please tell me."

I look up at the man, this man who's become like family to me most of the time. His face looks pained, like he's hurting because of this. The scar on his face doesn't even show in this light, but I can still see his torment. *He wants to help me. I should know this.*

I lean against his shoulder. "I'm sorry I panicked in DC. And just now."

I feel his arm around my shoulders, and it's a reassuring feeling. He squeezes me slightly. "It's okay, Alanna. Please, don't hold it in, tell me what's going on."

I look up at him, into those eyes where I first saw darkness and regret. The only thing I see in them now is concern … and love.

He makes me feel safe.

I sigh deeply. "I did … things … while I was in Hell."

He nods and pulls me closer. "What kinds of things?"

"Things I regret. I dreamed things, too."

He rocks me gently. "What kinds of things?"

He's persistent, trying to get some specifics out of me.

He makes me feel safe.

"I spent all that time down there, and it felt like it took forever to get to Dad. During the journey, I encountered trouble … I fell out of a boat and nearly drowned in the river Styx."

His face shows his concern. "Are you okay?"

"I wasn't, not after that, not by a long shot, because that's when the nightmares began. I had a vision … everyone was dying … you and Michi were … were together, and you hated me … and let the wendigo eat me …"

His eyes darken again. I reach a hand up to his scarred cheek.

"I know you really wouldn't but you have to understand … these visions felt so real to me … and especially after I wound up …" I start sniffling, and tears start falling. "After I started participating in torments for damned souls, I had more visions that you would reject me when I came back … that you wouldn't want me anymore … wouldn't love me anymore."

I'm degenerating into unintelligible blubbering. I clutch my legs tighter to my chest. William still has his arm around me.

"I'm such a horrible person, William. I don't deserve the Sword. I don't deserve you." I look up at him again, cheeks soaked. "I caused harm to souls. I destroyed souls. I'm no better than the demons …"

"No, Alanna, you're much better than the demons." He clutches me tight with both arms. "Is this why you freaked out at the White House?"

My eyes are squinted closed and I nod frantically. "I heard all those blueshirts screaming, and it brought Hell back to me, because that's all you ever hear is screams of terror and torment. It brought those visions back, and I got so scared of you … I thought you were

135

the wendigo of my vision, and I was afraid of being consumed ..." I lean into his shoulder. "I'm so sorry ..." I can't talk anymore. It's all I can do to sob loudly.

I feel his hand stroking my hair gently. "What were you afraid of?"

I sniffle and look up at him, speaking haltingly. "I was afraid ... that you didn't love me ... that you saw who I really was ... that you knew what I had done ... that when you wouldn't sit by me ... that you were done with me, that I'd hurt you too much."

"Never, Alanna. I've sworn my life to you, in my heart. There's no way I would ever hurt you, and likewise nothing you could do to hurt me that much."

My sobs are slowing down. I raise my head back up to see his face.

He's smiling. He's smiling widely, and right at me.

"Alanna, there's nothing you could ever do that will change the way I feel about you." He clutches me tightly into his arms, lifting me into his lap. "I love you, Alanna. Don't ever doubt that."

I bring a hand up to his unscarred cheek. "I love you too, William." I lay my head on his shoulder. He pulls me tighter into his arms and rocks me, calming me. Before I know it, I hear his voice again ... soft at first, but melodic.

> *My days are brighter than morning air*
> *Evergreen pine and autumn dew*
> *But all my days were twice as fair*
> *If I could share my days with you*

Memories come back, memories of years before, of recovering from a grievous wound, of learning of William's existence ... of learning of his feelings for me, which he had been harboring for years. My hand rests on his chest as he continues.

My nights are warmer than fire coals
Incense and stars and smoke bamboo
But nights were warm beyond compare
If I could share my nights with you …

His voice is calming, relaxing me down to my very soul. All of the worries are starting to melt away, being lost in the flow of his voice.

To dance in my dreams
To shine when I need the sun
With you to hold me when dreams are done
And oh, my dearest love
If you would take my love
Then all my dreams are truly begun …

His voice drops lower, quieter, into a richer tone. I'm suddenly aware of his gaze on me, his eyes glistening in the dim light of my room.

And time weaves ribbons of memory
To sweeten life when youth is through
But I would need no memories there
If I could share
My life with you.

I close my eyes and sink deeper into this ring of comfort that's been built around me. My voice falters as I whisper. "Thank you, William."

He smiles widely at me. "Don't thank me yet. There's a reason I was talking to your dad today." He reaches into his shirt pocket …

… and it comes out with a small gold ring with a chip of a green stone as a setting at the top.

Is he doing what I think he's doing?!

"We're going to be so busy over the next month, I'm afraid the time's never going to come. So I was asking

137

him this morning if this would be okay, and he gave me the go-ahead." He takes my left hand and places it on his chest with the hand holding the ring. "Alanna, my time here without you, these past two years, they were hard for me. It was hard to wake up every morning and know your face wasn't there, I couldn't see you smile, hear your voice, look into your eyes, or even tell you how much I loved you. Every night I prayed to the Creator that you were safe, and that you would come back. I made a pledge in my heart to be yours, no matter what changes happened to you or me."

I'm shuddering again, for a completely different reason. *My heart is pounding so hard right now.*

"When you came back, that was the happiest day of my life, and I decided then and there that I never wanted to be apart from you, ever again, in this world or any other." He clutches me tighter around my waist with the other arm, and I'm instantly aware of the feel of his body, the warmth we're sharing in this moment. His eyes work their way to mine, and the love is clear in them. "Alanna Ariel Sharpe, I am humbly asking if you would do me the honor of marrying me."

I think I'm hyperventilating. My mind is racing, trying to find any reason to say "no." *We might die in three months. If we win, we'll have to find a way to start a life together. Any children we have will have a lot of supernatural blood to deal with. Even though the calendar says I'm nineteen, I'm only seventeen in mind.*

Those reasons get snuffed out by two things. William's face has an anticipatory expression, which shows how much he loves me and how much he missed me ... and how much I missed him, too.

Eventually, one thought drowns out the cacophony of disagreement in my brain.

He's loved you almost his entire life. You've loved him nearly that long. Admit it, you were over the moon when he danced with you in Oklahoma City, and that feeling came back when he sang to you at the Refuge … and just now. Love like this is rare. Don't pass it up when you have the chance to make it forever.

My eyes meet William's once more. My voice doesn't speak, but my lips make out the words. "Yes, I will."

The ring slides easily on my hand. The green stone radiates with an interesting reflection off of the light pouring into the room from the open door. If I hadn't cried out all my tears earlier, there'd be joyful ones to share right now. As it is, my heart's drumming in my ears as I clutch my arms tightly around William's neck and kiss him with abandon.

Grasping at my happiness while I have the chance. After all, we may be dead this time in three months.

Chapter Fourteen: Alliances

July 21st

The morning greets me once more with the anticipation of another day. The nervousness of yesterday is slightly tempered by the events of last night. In the pale daylight I lift up my left hand.

It's still there. The ring's right there, staring back at me.

It was real. I'm engaged. William asked me to marry him, and I agreed. Wow.

My heart lightens slightly, and I sit up in the bed, ready to start my day. The good news being that today isn't my turn to train our impromptu army: that pleasure falls to Teresa, and I'm praying for her. I throw on some clothes and head down to the dining room for breakfast.

Interestingly, William isn't there yet. Did he decide to sleep in, I wonder? The thought doesn't stay for long as my eyes spot Michi's orange fur sitting at the table, and my body gravitates toward her. I grab a plate on my way over and sit down next to her.

She seems cheerful this morning. "What's happening?" I ask.

"Oh not much. I think I've got the spell figured out."

I'm confused. "The spell?"

She flashes me a meaningful look. "You know … *that* spell … the one involving fire …?"

The realization hits. *She thinks she can contact Fahaian.* "Gotcha. Let's try it out after breakfast, what do you say?"

Michi nods enthusiastically, just as Mom and Dad walk up to the table with their own plates and mugs. Dad is the first to break into the conversation, and his words are enough to make me blush. "So Alanna, let's see it."

Michi's expression changes quickly. "See what?"

I'm madly blushing now. Kind of quietly, I answer, "This." I lift my left hand up and place it at the middle of the table.

Dad's smile crosses his whole face, and Mom's expression lightens. "Is this from William?"

I nod. "He asked last night."

Michi hugs my shoulders and shrieks right in my ear, bouncing us both slightly. "Omigod omigod omigod! That's awesome, Alanna!" I'm now very self-conscious of all the attention, considering Michi's shriek has just drawn the attention of everyone in this room and the next three over. She leans over and takes a closer look at the ring. "What kind of stone is that? I've never seen green like that before …"

Dad chuckles. "William told me, it's a Petoskey stone from his original hometown. This apparently was his mother's wedding ring." He looks over my hand closely and raises an eyebrow. "Huh, he said it wasn't resized, but it looks like it was made for you."

I'm surprised by that myself. "Well, I wasn't really paying attention … it was kind of an emotional moment, as you can imagine."

Mom smiles and nods knowingly. "Congratulations. I hope you're as happy with William as your father

141

and I have been." She leans her head gently on Dad's shoulder.

Michi's leaning her head on one hand now, gazing at all of us with kind of a dreamy expression on her face. "Damn, you guys are all so cute ..." She sighs deeply.

I know exactly what will cheer her up. I stand up and pat her on the shoulder. "Come on, Michi, let's try out that spell, okay?"

She readily agrees, grabbing her own plate and standing up with me. Once all of our breakfast dishes are taken care of, we make our way into the great room of the Ranch house, where a roaring fire is already going in the fireplace. Michi takes a position directly in front of the blazing flames.

"What was the block?" I ask her idly.

"Huh? Oh, it turns out that the fire can't be started by magic means. I re-read a lot of the books Fahaian left behind, and most of them mentioned natural fire being the holy symbol of his faith. So I thought about it, and realized that I'd used the gauntlet to start our campfire in Virginia." She makes a motion toward the fireplace. "Mom insists that this fire never be magical in nature, because she doesn't like the unpredictability of magic fire. You remember eight years ago?"

"Yeah, I do." The Ranch had a massive fire that nearly destroyed the entire house, and as it was scorched three acres' worth of land.

"That was caused by Dad burning trash with magic fire. Because of that, Mom forbade magic fire from the house."

Seems like Aunt Kitty forbids an awful lot of stuff in the Salem household. "Okay, so natural fire is the key, you think?"

"Pretty sure. Here goes." Michi raises the gauntlet toward the fireplace, as her cat's ears turn backward. Her almond-pupil eyes narrow as her concentration level increases. I look over at the fire and see the sparks beginning to appear again, like they did near Arlington. It looks like this is going to be another failed attempt …

The fire changes colors abruptly, from orange to dark red. It flares up into the chimney like a gas burner turned up too high. The heat radiating out of the hearth almost reminds me of the volcanoes, and Pele's home in Hawaii.

Then there's a barely-perceptible voice, echoing in the deepest corners of my mind. =*Hello?*=

I look over at Michi. She simply grins.

The voice calls again. =*Hello?*=

Michi clears her throat. "Fahaian? Can you hear me?"

The voice's words change in my head. =*Faintly. Is that you, Michika?*=

The tears are threatening in Michi's eyes. "It's me, yeah. I think I got the knack of this fire thing you were teaching me."

That's a bit of a surprise. Fahaian was teaching this to Michi? I thought he was the only one who could do things with fire.

The voice begins chuckling. =*You have done well, my dear. What news is there?*=

Michi motions toward me, asking me to speak I think. I clear my throat. "Your Majesty, it's Alanna."

143

The voice takes on the tone of relief. It's getting even clearer now, and for sure I can tell it's Fahaian now. =*Please, Alanna, everyone else calls me Your Majesty, but for you I am still Fahaian. It is a great pleasure to hear your voice once more.*=

"Thank you, Fahaian. I've missed you too, but I doubt as much as Michi has."

A brief pause. =*Or as much as I've missed Michi.*=

Now I know things have progressed, if we're both using the same pet name for Michi.

"I wish we could use this conversation just to catch up, but there's serious business right now. Can you talk in confidence?" I swallow hard waiting for the response.

=*I only have people here that I trust. You don't have to worry.*=

"Good." I look over at Michi, then back to the fire. "The Regents are making their next major move in three months. They're planning to attack the Ranch directly and destroy Avalon. If they succeed, all supernaturals around the world will die."

Silence. I think he's trying to take in the information. =*I heard that President Regent died.*=

Michi pipes up in the conversation. "Yeah, but it looks like it was Jennifer pulling the strings the whole time, and she's the bitch getting ready to attack. She's going to try to kill us all in one fell swoop, and she's massing the entire SSA for this attack."

=*I see. What do you need of me?*=

It's my turn. "We'll mostly need some reinforcements. We only have about 300 to defend the Ranch with, against 20 entire SSA troops."

=*That is a significant tactical disadvantage. I will muster my troops for you.*=

144

"I appreciate it, but there's one other thing you need to do for us."

=Absolutely, Alanna, anything you need.=

I clear my throat, looking back briefly to where the Operation Glass Jaw file lies on the living room table, then turn back to the fire. "Part of the operation involves SSA deep cover agents around the world 'fighting off' supernatural attacks in all the United Nations capitals. I'd venture a guess that they have some in Amman as well. They're going to have demons attack the capitals for the SSA agents to fight … so we'll need your help to find the demons and destroy them before the attacks take place."

A brief moment of silence. *=I now have the phones of several world leaders, particularly the Super 15 nations. If we can get a chain of calls going, I believe we can accomplish this for you, Alanna. We must not allow the New Empire to spread around the world.=*

It's nice to have a king on our side. "Great. I appreciate the help a lot." My heart feels a lot lighter after this conversation.

=Michi?=

I can still hear Fahaian, but I know he's directing his words to my best friend. She leans closer to the fire, a longing expression on her face. "Yes, Fahaian, I'm here."

=Michi, I am sorry I have not been able to get back to you sooner. I still stand by my promise, to come back to your side.=

"I hope when you do that you're still happy about it, though. There's been changes."

=I have spoken with Durga, Michi. I know.=

Michi's face goes as pale as it can beneath her fur. "Oh God, you do?"

145

Fahaian chuckles. =*You have no need to worry, Michi. Your soul never changes. It is your soul which makes you who you are, not your body. I do not care if you have been turned into a giant cat, or inanimate gas, or a tree. I still feel the way I do. I love you, Michi, and want you as my queen.*=

Tears are streaking down Michi's furry cheeks. "You mean it?"

The fire takes on a different shape. To both of our surprise, the flames start forming a head, then a recognizable face.

Fahaian grins at us through a flaming avatar. =*With all my heart I mean it, Michi. I love you.*=

Michi approaches the fiery visage, tears streaming with abandon. "I love you too." She reaches her head toward the fire. The tiger girl and the fiery head share a tender kiss, with no signs of discomfort coming from my best friend. In fact, she's giggling slightly as she draws back. "Come back to me soon, okay?"

=*I will, in force. Alanna, you can count on me.*=

"Thanks a lot, Fahaian." I smile as the face retreats back into the fireplace, then the flames turn back into regular old fire once more. Michi's looking utterly twitterpated as she sits back on the floor, a silly grin plastered across her face. I could make a Cheshire Cat joke here, but I doubt she'd even understand it right now.

She finally looks up at me, eyes shimmering, the grin never leaving her face. "Queen Michika ... I like the sound of that!"

I stand up and help Michi to her feet. "Try this on for size ... 'Presenting Their Royal Highnesses, King Fahaian and Queen Michika of Jordan.'"

The giggling is unstoppable now between the two of us. It's been so long since we've been allowed to just be *girls.*

Chapter Fifteen: War Council

August 8th

I stand proudly at the window of the Ranch house and watch a mini-skirmish taking place in the field outside. Two groups of fighters from the Attack division are facing each other down. One of them is in torn blue t-shirts, given to them by Gabe: this is a strategy session, and they're supposed to be the SSA, and as such can only use guns and not their powers. The other side is using their powers to the full advantage.

A few faces I recognize in the crowd. Lydia Dales is using a trick I taught her to take advantage of her power, rushing up behind opponents and covering their faces with her hands, force-feeding them her wine and incapacitating them. Trent Gracin rolls across the field and bowls into a group of "blueshirts," knocking them all aside. A couple others I remember from their demonstrations, such as Harry Tyner, a sound specialist who vibrates his arms like a cricket's legs and creates sound wave attacks. By the end of the exercise, the "blueshirt" force is scattered and beaten, and only a couple of the supernatural team have any wear.

Gabe walks into the center of the field and claps. I can't exactly hear what he's telling them, but I'm sure it has something to do with countering the part of the SSA playbook he was showing them.

My army, now they're truly becoming one.

"Alanna?"

A gentle voice behind me turns my attention away. It's Mom, looking even better as the days go along. She's smiling, but I also see she's holding her uniform I wore through the Inferno, the one that I thought I had destroyed, but now is somehow just as clean as it was the first time I put it on.

"Kitty tells me you've been wearing my uniform for a while."

I'm kind of bashful for some reason. "I hope you don't mind, it was useful for being able to use my wings without ripping holes in shirts."

Mom nods kind of sadly. "What about your … other transformations?"

I sigh deeply. I know it makes her very depressed that I can grow into a dragon now too, but I'm determined to make that curse into a benefit for us all, just like she has. "It works with those too, just like Uncle Cyrus said it worked with yours."

She sighs and smiles again. "Good. I'm very glad it still works." She turns around and starts walking back down the hallway. I can't resist, I follow her. We wind up at the room that for two years held my comatose father; he's now sharing it with his wife, which is certainly proper.

Then I notice Mom taking off her shirt. "Mom, what are you doing?"

She slips on the uniform top. "Still fits. Amazing." She turns around toward me. "We need to take a look at your dragon, and see exactly what she's capable of."

I shrug. "I've been finding that out myself for a while, actually. I …" I stop myself short because I realize it's not for my benefit. It's for *hers*. "Okay. I'm running out of outfits, though."

149

"Don't worry." Mom reaches down by the bed, then tosses me a mass of fabric. "Cyrus has you covered."

It's purple and turquoise blue, and it feels much the same as the uniform. I hold up the top and find that it's made to the same design as the uniform, but smaller, which means it'll fit me a bit better than the uniform did.

Then there's the final touch. In the same space on the top where Mom's maiden name is stitched on the uniform is mine. White embroidery forms SHARPE in military block letters.

"Put that on and meet me outside. We'll fly." Mom punctuates her words with a loving smile.

Oh God, I haven't flown with Mom in what feels like forever! I rush back down to my room and quickly change into the flight suit. When I emerge, Mom's already waiting for me at the front door of the house.

I'm suddenly caught by the way she looks. Sure, she might be in her fifties, but the uniform still fits her, and she still looks as young as ever. If there's one thing Gerard wasn't able to do, it was destroy her spirit. I get an image in my mind of Mom and Dad and Uncle Cyrus and Aunt Kitty in their adventuring days, fighting off demons, making life a living hell for anyone who challenged them.

Now that duty falls to their daughters. Michi and myself.

"Are you coming?" She sounds giddy, like she's been wanting to fly with me as much as I have with her.

"You got it, Mom!" I rush over to her and we both run out the front door. Once we're at a clearing near the door, Mom waves me aside and closes her eyes, beginning her transformation. This always fascinates me to watch, seeing my mother change from a tall green-skinned woman into a gigantic dragon. Her neck lengthens, her torso bulks up and her limbs become legs with sharp talons. Her wings sprout and grow to immense proportions.

The dragon stands before me finally, and I can kind of see a smile on her snout. *"Your turn."*

It *is* my turn, isn't it? I do much like Mom did, close my eyes and focus all my concentration on my body. I feel the changes take place, the stretching of sinew and bone and ligament, pulling my proportions out to the extreme that the dragon would display. I feel my tail sprout, pushing its way from my spine; I feel my wings stretching far over me; I feel my neck and my face lengthening. I finally open my eyes when I sense every change is finished.

I'm eye-to-eye with Mom now. She takes one pacing look-over of my dragon body. I flap my wings, a little bit of showing off on my part. I hear her snuffle as she looks over my dragon's haunches, my wings, and even my tail, which is a difference from her own body. It would make me self-conscious, but this is Mom we're talking about. I'd imagine she wants to know what Gerard did to me and how it compares to what he did to her.

When she seems satisfied, she comes back around to face me. She flaps her wings a couple times, lifts up to her rear haunches, and leaps. A hard downward flap of her wings launches her high into the sky, and she glides over my head.

Far be it for me to leave her alone up there! I decide I'm going to try her technique for takeoff: I stretch my wings a little bit, then lift up on my rear legs. The tail

151

helps me to stabilize my posture. I might be overthinking it, but I'm trying to coordinate my jump and my flap, as she seemed to do. Finally, I just decide to do it.

I jump and flap. My body rockets up into the air, just like hers. I begin my swimmer's stroke wing flaps, and join her in an easy circling glide over the Ranch. At this altitude, we can see the surrounding area where the place is currently parked, such as the Edmonton skyline and the rolling plains of Alberta and Manitoba.

My gaze winds up fixed on Mom, still gliding in lazy circles. She flaps her wings and ascends, then starts accelerating. I angle myself so that I can pursue her, beginning my regular fast wing pattern. I find that I'm catching up to her very quickly, to the point that I nearly overshoot her, except I slow up at the last minute to fly alongside her. We turn and bank, creating lazy figure-eights in the air, dipping and chasing each other.

Mom nods toward me, then turns away, opens her maw, and sends a firecast blazing into the afternoon air. Her face turns back toward me.

She wants to see me do it, too. I flap faster to come alongside her, and then let fly with my own pillar of flames. The range is similar, but mine is a narrower, fine-tuned beam, as opposed to Mom's, which spreads out and covers a lot of area in a short period of time.

She seems impressed. She nods at me, then begins a decent down to the ground. I follow her, and together we alight and land in the same clearing from which we started. A moment's concentration later, we're both shrinking back down into our human forms, until we're face-to-face once again, mother and daughter.

The adrenaline is still high for both of us. We clutch each other tightly.

"I'm so proud of you, Alanna. It's a terrible burden, but you've done so much and so well …"

It feels good to receive this praise. "Thanks, Mom." I snuggle closer into her embrace.

Our hug is interrupted by a male voice clearing his throat behind us. I turn and see William standing there. "Ladies, Alanna is needed inside. Gabe asked for you."

I nod to my fiancé … call me silly, but it's really nice to think of him that way … but I squeeze Mom's hand. "We'll fly again soon, I promise."

She smiles kind of sadly. "I know we will, Alanna. When this is over, we'll glide in skies of glory."

That sounds far too ominous. Come on, let's keep some optimism here!

I squeeze Mom's hand one last time before crossing the plain to join William at the door. He takes an arm and wraps it around my waist.

"So what's going on?" I ask.

"I don't really know. Gabe seems pretty enthused about his strategy session today, and he told us he wants all of us trainers to meet."

I nod. "It's very hard to figure out what he's thinking most of the time."

"Agreed," William responds with a low voice. "I've never met such an enigmatic man in my life."

If only you knew the half of it!

We make our way into the dining room, where all the other trainers are seated around the table. Gabe stands at the head, while Teresa and Aunt Kitty flank him. Michi sits with Teresa while Uncle Cyrus is next

153

to his wife, holding her hand. I don't think they've even let go of them at all when they're together lately, and considering the stakes I really don't blame them.

Gabe motions for me and William to sit down. I take the opposite end of the table from Gabe, and William puts himself to my left side, claiming my hand in his once he sits down.

"Thank you for joining me here, folks. I'd like an update on your training." He motions to Teresa. "Let's start with you."

Teresa takes a deep breath. "With the exception of the rescued SSA supernaturals, most of our forces are terribly out of shape. I'm doing my best with them, but I think we'll be lucky if we don't have half the force having heart attacks before the SSA even crosses the fence lines."

Gabe nods. "Unfortunate, but we need to work with what we've got. How much improvement have you seen out of them?"

"Little victories here and there, but not very much. It's all about stamina, really, the staying power of our troops leaves something to be desired."

"I see." Gabe turns toward the next trainer. "Michika, what's the word?"

"We've got a good amount of battle mages, which we can send out for distance attacks and the like, but don't count on them getting too physical. Most of them can't take a punch without wilting like one of Mom's soufflés."

"Anyone who's better in the physical department?"

"A couple, myself included, but I'd strongly recommend keeping most of them toward the back of the lines."

Gabe nods. "I see. Kitty?"

Aunt Kitty clears her throat. "Most of them are taking well to firearms training. I got a couple real marksmen among the Support team, so I'd like to place them up top as snipers. Small arms is what most of the others are accustomed to, so they'll stick with the pistols and slingshots."

We all get disbelieving looks on our faces. Gabe's expression barely shivers. "Slingshots? You aren't serious, are you?"

"Deadly serious. If it's good enough for David, it's for damn sure good enough for our forces."

Silence dominates the room, until Gabe breaks it. "Okay then. William, your report please."

William squeezes my hand. "Our medics are getting the best that I can give, but too many of them have too little experience with field triage. If we get into an especially brutal fight, they'll be overwhelmed, and it'll be a difficult thing to get our side back in fighting shape."

"I see." Gabe presses forward. "Cyrus?"

"I think the door's going to be in good hands. I hand-picked the eight highest-skilled members of our force, and gave them the duty of guarding the door. Among the defenders will be myself and Kitty." Aunt Kitty squeezes his hand as he says this. "I've given the other defenders a crash course in Avalon's importance, and emphasized exactly how vital it is that the SSA not cross through it."

"How much of the stakes do they know?"

"Only as much as I've told them, which isn't very much."

155

Gabe nods. "That brings us to you, Alanna, what have you to report?"

It's my turn to clutch to William's hand tightly. "I've been giving some of our forces some alternative means of using their powers, which they're taking to pretty easily. I think you saw a couple of those options in your scrimmage today, Gabe."

"Yes, I did notice some interesting things going on."

"Many of the latents are starting to fully realize their powers, so we should have a fully supernatural force by the time we need it."

"And that gets us to the point of this meeting," Gabe announces. I'm dreading this. "Ladies and gentlemen, you've done well in the short period of time you've had thus far, but now things have to accelerate."

Worried murmurs circle the table. "Accelerate by how much?" William asks.

"By a tremendous amount, and here's why." Gabe tosses the file on Operation Glass Jaw on the table. "I've finished my review of this report and battle plan. It's very thorough, indeed, right down to the projected location of the Ranch in October."

We lean in eagerly, awaiting Gabe's continuation.

"Cyrus, please confirm if this is correct. Glass Jaw is set to commence on October 27th, at which time they've forecast the Ranch to appear 50 miles east of Boise, Idaho."

Uncle Cyrus closes his eyes, thinking it over in his head. His face drops when he answers. "They're only off by about half a mile, but yes that's where the Ranch will be on that date."

"Wait a minute," I interrupt. "How do we know for sure? Why would we even be moving in the first place? We're in Canada, the New Empire can't touch us."

"Normally, I'd agree," Gabe intones, "but now with the focus on placing pressure on the UN, Canada can't afford to be defiant toward its neighbor anymore. I've heard from reliable sources that SSA troops are headed into Alberta, looking for us."

"Because of this," Uncle Cyrus continues, "I'm setting up a spell which will send the Ranch to random locations around North America at random intervals. This way, we can stay one step ahead of the SSA. Unfortunately, someone's managed to calculate the randomness of the spell, and figured out a pattern which is pretty accurate."

"That's right," Gabe confirms. "And as such, we need to accelerate our preparations." He leans forward on the dining room table. "Ladies, gentlemen, I propose that we move up the schedule of Operation Glass Jaw, and drop in on the SSA early … say, two months early."

He can't be serious! That's suicide! Everyone around the table launches into an uproar. We're all pretty much agreed, there's no way the supernaturals will be battle-ready on that kind of a timeline.

Teresa stands up to Gabe. "What you're asking is impossible!"

"You might think so," Gabe cautions, "but I don't. I saw how they're working together out there today. They have strategy, when they have an able field commander to give it to them. They have ability. They have powers at their disposal. Most of all, they have the will to fight. They know that the stakes are very

157

high, that their very existence depends on winning this battle. I have every confidence in these people that they *will* pull it together, that they *will* work for you, and in the end they *will* defeat the SSA."

Somehow Gabe's assurance is less than satisfying. "Are you absolutely sure about this?"

Gabe smirks. "Positive. If we do this, victory is ours."

He truly believes in this plan of attack. He wants to bring the battle to them, not wait around for them to come to us.

I think I'd want to do the same thing.

"Okay, Gabe. You got me." I stand up at my end of the table. "I'll get their powers working to the fullest."

William rises next to me. "We'll have the best field hospital we can muster."

Michi stands. "Our mages will be ready to go kick some blueshirt ass."

Both Uncle Cyrus and Aunt Kitty rise in unison. Aunt Kitty speaks for them both. "You have my guns and Cy's defenders."

Teresa's face appears bewildered, but finally she stands with us. "Well, I can't promise anything, but I'll do my best to make sure nobody drops dead on us."

Gabe smiles. "It's settled, then. One way or another, in nineteen days this war *ends.*"

Chapter Sixteen: Final Lull

August 24th

This is my last chance to make sure these people are ready to fight. It's their last shot to show me what they've got.

Today's training session moves along almost too quickly, with our forces blasting away at each other trying to capture the flag. I've arranged this exercise for the entire Attack division, to train them to go after the main command center, and to improvise a means to get there using their powers. I'm quite satisfied with the work I'm seeing out there, especially from the SSA-trained fighters. Trent and Teresa are working well as a coherent team: Teresa sets up her opponents while Trent knocks them down.

I wouldn't expect less from those two. When they arrived, they had been in a relationship while brainwashed in the SSA, a relationship they chose to continue. Now after a month training in the use of their powers, I'm very happy in how they use each other to complement attacks. The same is true of several small teams within the Attack division, who've found they have compatible supernatural abilities and have started creating combined attacks.

My thoughts are interrupted when I hear a whoop rise from one end of the field. I look toward my left and see that Isaac Portland is holding up and waving the green flag, the one for the opposing side. The game is over. I draw everyone's attention with applause, as the setting sun begins to frame them all in tones of gold and orange.

"Well done, everyone. I've seen a lot of progress being made since those first few days. You're definitely ready to fight."

"And win, right?" one voice calls out from the middle of the crowd.

Can I promise them that? I have a moment of doubt, which doesn't last very long. "Fight *and* win!"

A loud cheer erupts from the group. I raise my hands and motion for quiet.

"Folks, as you've probably heard, in three days' time we are taking the fight directly to the SSA. I was tasked with making sure all of you were fully able to use your abilities, and carry out our battle plan to your fullest capability. I'm happy to report that you all have passed this test. All of you have learned methods of using your powers that stretch every definition of them. You've made me proud in this regard."

Another cheer. They won't like the next part of this speech … *I* don't even like it, and I've been rehearsing it for days.

"I'm not going to lie to you. Some of you will go into battle and never return. Many of you may be hurt in one way or another. Just know that you sacrifice yourselves for a greater cause, for a greater mission. By fighting, you ensure that the New Empire of America can not, and by God will not, ever target another supernatural for extermination. By fighting, you ensure that a once free nation will become free once more, that the free world will remain free of the Regents' tyranny. By laying your lives on the line, you will be ensuring that others may live."

Quiet murmurs rustle through the crowd.

"I will be out there fighting alongside you all. I will take the risk with you, as will all of your trainers and allies. When this battle ends, we shall all stand together in the glow of justice served!"

My wings unfurl as I enunciate the final words of my speech. This causes another eruption of cheers.

I'm so uncomfortable right now ...

I dismiss the assemblage and turn around. Behind me, William and Michi are applauding as well.

"Great speech, Alanna," William says kind of playfully.

"Awe-inspiring!" Michi chimes.

"Oh shut up, guys, you know I hate speaking." I take my best friend and my fiancé under my arms in a group hug and lead them back inside the Ranch house. Once inside, though, they team up and pull me aside.

"Listen, we had an idea, and we wanted to know if you'd be in with us," Michi starts out.

"I'm listening."

William smiles. "We'd like to throw a birthday party for your mom. I know it's the night before we're going to fight, but it'll be a chance for everyone to have one last night of fun before we all go into danger."

My mind races back in time, to three years ago and another impromptu birthday party organized by William, only that time it was my sixteenth.

Things have gone so far since then ... it's one of my happiest memories of recent times.

I twist the ring gently. "Sure. I think it's a great idea."

Michi hugs me tightly. "Great! Let me tell Mom then!" She runs off in the general direction of the dining room, leaving me and William alone.

"Just like a few years ago," I idly comment.

"Yes it is, except this time we have a greater celebration. Your family is reunited, that's reason enough for a party, but there's also the birthday, and the wedding …"

Wait, wedding?! "William, is there something you're not telling me …?"

"Huh?" He seems genuinely confused. "Oh, you mean …" He points back and forth between the two of us. I have to admit, it's kind of cute to make him this uncomfortable. "Sorry, I should've explained more. I forgot to tell you that Trent and Teresa got engaged while you were gone, and they want to get married before the battle."

I nod knowingly. "I certainly understand that. I'll be more than happy to share Mom's birthday party with a wedding reception."

William returns my smile with a gentle kiss. "I'd better help the Salems get things ready. It's going to be a huge party." He stands up, but lingers gently while holding my hand in his, lightly fingering the ring on my finger. "I love you, Alanna."

I squeeze his hand. "I love you too." He runs off, leaving me alone with my thoughts and a roaring fireplace.

We're only three days out from a conflict … one that we're looking for, a fight we're trying to pick … that will determine the fate of an entire population of people on the face of the planet. Should we fail, should we fall, there's nothing to stop Avalon from dying, and all supernaturals around the world from joining its fate.

I look up at a mirror positioned above the mantel of the fireplace. There I am, the girl with the wings and the Sword. The one that Gabe expects to lead everyone to victory; the girl who only four years ago was more concerned with passing her midterm math test than commanding an army. My eyes focus on the features of my face, to look for any signs that this time has taken its toll on me. Dark circles are threatening beneath my eyes, no doubt from the long sleepless nights I've endured. I look a little skinnier than I did before the SSA took Mom, possibly a result of fasting for eighteen days in the Inferno but I think it's more likely because stress is the ultimate diet drug.

I take a closer look at myself. This is the girl that William fell in love with so many years ago, on a dance floor in Oklahoma City. This is the face he kisses almost every day and every night. This is the woman he asked to marry him.

Most importantly, this is the girl who agreed to it.

So much change has taken place, it's enough to make a person's head spin right off their shoulders. I clutch the Sword's hilt tightly, feeling its reassuring heft, its slightly warm metallic feel under my hand. This is my birthright, along with my wings. These make me who I am in the eyes of my forces, and in the eyes of those who would destroy me.

But they're not all there is to me. These are merely small symbols, compared to the heart and soul who wields them.

In three days, this girl might be gone, along with every other supernatural. In three days, this girl might be triumphant, and lead us all into a new era without the New Empire of America.

However it plays out, though, one thing is clear. No matter what happens to me, or to William or Michi or any of us, I will not let this conflict change who I am at heart. I will not allow this fight to turn me into that which I wage war against. I will stay true to my heart, to my friends, to those that I love dearly.

One way or another, I'll be with Mom and Dad … and William … forever.

August 26th

There's only a short training session this morning, and thankfully I'm not the one who's leading it. Michi has the mages one last time, putting them through their paces. She's training them this morning to do collaborative spells, which can do anything from blast opponents to raise shields. That's what she tells me, anyway.

My mind is a million miles away from battle preparations. I'm more concerned with happy things this morning, and I'm helping Aunt Kitty and Uncle Cyrus with the last preparations for today's party. We're just putting up the last of the crepe streamers across the ceiling of the living room when Michi rushes in.

"We're done for the day!"

I smile down at her. "Great, can you give us a hand here?"

She smirks and raises her gauntleted hand. *"Lift."*

The remaining coils of crepe streamers rise off of the floor, unroll, and create festive criss-crosses across the ceiling. I climb down off of the ladder I'm using and join Michi at ground level.

"Looks good."

"It better, this is going to be the party of the century and I don't want it to be in a dull looking room."

I hug Michi, knowing she means only the best. "It won't be, I'm confident of that."

Michi grins and turns back to decorating, lifting more streamers off the floor. I go into the kitchen, where Aunt Kitty's standing over a stove.

"Anything I can do to help?" I offer.

She looks back at me and smiles. "Not much, really, I'm just about done here. Why don't you go get your folks and bring 'em out? We'll bet getting started in a few."

I'm kind of depressed that I'm not able to help more, but I acquiesce, heading down the hallway to Mom and Dad's room. I hear their voices as I approach the cracked-open door.

"… they're going to be outmatched, aren't they?"

Mom's question worries me, but Dad comes in and that makes matters worse. "Unfortunately. I'm afraid for them all, but especially for Alanna. I hope she's able to handle defeat."

"She's become a very confident young woman."

"I agree, but I think sometimes she expects to win every time." Dad sighs deeply. "I just want her to be okay, to survive this. There must be a Guardsman, no matter what."

I close my eyes with my hand on the door, ready to push it open. I don't want to be too emotional.

Mom's voice comes back and pushes me over the emotional ledge. "She will, Cole. She'll make it. She's a

Sharpe, after all, and your family … *our* family … has a habit of being incredibly hard to kill."

Even as tears threaten, I smile because Mom's so confident in me. *Thank you, Mom.* I push the door open gently while knocking on it. "Hey guys, they're ready for you."

Mom and Dad turn and look at me. They've been cuddling on the edge of the bed, it looks like for a while. Mom smiles at me. "We're coming, Alanna." They both stand up and come up to me, opening the door wider.

We walk down the hallway arm-in-arm, the three of us, with Mom and Dad on either side of me. *I can't help but feel like I'm walking this corridor for the last time …*

When we reach the end of the hallway, coming out into the dining room, the place is filled from wall to wall with our supernatural forces, and even some of the ones who were too badly hurt to contribute to the fight. All of them raise a cheer as we enter.

Then it occurs to me, next to none of these people has seen Mom yet.

"Ladies and gentlemen," Michi's voice rises above the din, "allow me to introduce to you the Sharpe family! Cole Sharpe, the Penitent! Ariel Sharpe, the dragon! And Alanna Sharpe, the Guardsman!"

A loud cheer rises from the entire group, followed by a mass singing of "Happy Birthday" to Mom. The mood is immediately festive, and I know it's only going to get more so the longer this party goes on.

When the din has settled, a more reverent mood rushes over the entire crowd as another group of people step out of the hallway. We quickly move aside as Trent and Teresa, dressed in the best wedding regalia they could find at the Ranch, step past, walking down an improvised aisle to the end where Gabe waits, a small book in his hand. They stop at the end, before Gabe, who opens the book and begins officiating their wedding.

"Dearly beloved, supernatural family, we gather here in this place to join this man, Trent Gracin, and this woman, Teresa Iles, in one of the holiest covenants on Earth, the bonds of marriage. God willing, marriage entails many responsibilities and promises …"

It's a very simple, heartfelt ceremony. I look around me and see a few other couples as Gabe continues. Michi's in a corner, hugging herself and clearly missing Fahaian. Mom and Dad stand next to me, their hands clutched together, looking lost in memory. I feel a warm presence walk up on my other side, and soon William's hand has wrapped around my own, close to me. All attention, though, is firmly on the couple at the front, who are now getting their opportunity to speak.

"Do you, Trent Howard Gracin, take this woman, Teresa Katherine Iles, as your lawfully wedded wife, to have and to hold, in sickness and in health, for richer or poorer, 'til death do you part?"

I get a chill at the last words Gabe intones. *Death could be a day away …*

Trent takes a deep breath, his eyes focused on Teresa. "I do."

Gabe smiles widely. "And do you, Teresa Katherine Iles, take this man, Trent Howard Gracin, as your lawfully wedded husband, to have and to hold, in sickness and in health, for richer or poorer, 'til death do you part?"

Teresa looks as nervous as anyone ever has, to my eye. She's clearly thinking like I am, but those thoughts are being overridden by her feelings for Trent. She clutches his hands a little tighter and whispers, "I do."

Gabe closes the book. "Then therefore by the power vested in me by my Employer, by the Hidden-In-Plain-Sight Ranch, and by the forces of life, I proclaim you to be husband and wife, as testified by all witnesses present." He does something unusual for him … wraps his arms around both Trent and Teresa, giving them a gentle hug, before turning them around to face the group. "Ladies and gentlemen, allow me to introduce to you Mr. and Mrs. Trent and Teresa Gracin!"

More cheering erupts from all of us.

"Oh, whoops, one last thing," Gabe interrupts over the din. "You may now kiss the bride!"

Trent pulls Teresa close to him, kissing her as best as he can with his insectoid face. When the two of them separate, he exhales a brief puff of frosty breath. The crowd goes even crazier.

The party continues as a celebration, both of Mom and the newly married couple. A lot of festive talk goes around, a lot of music is played, and an incredible amount of dancing livens up the event. I make my way through the group, getting handshakes and brief conversation, but making sure to check in on some particular people.

One person I check on is Ward Gregory, the White House spokesman we "captured." He seems to be adjusting well, having taken on the job of housekeeping around the Ranch house. He tells me that he's developed a rapport with Aunt Kitty, who's taken him under her wing and apparently started teaching him to shoot, something he wasn't sure he could do. He seems awfully happy to be away from the Regents, almost like he was conscripted or coerced into being their spokesman.

That seems so much like the Regents.

Another individual I check in with is Samuel Urich, who William tells me is developing into a fine field medic. He takes the opportunity to apologize to me for our first contentious meeting, and for doubting my supernatural abilities. While I appreciate the sentiment, it feels to me like I don't really need it … if he does his job during the battle tomorrow and nobody dies, that will be apology enough for me. He offers me a drink, but I politely decline. My eyes scan the room, looking around at the men's faces.

There he is. William is chatting with Dad and Uncle Cyrus along one wall. They seem to be having a good time, at least. I look to another side of the room, and there's Aunt Kitty and Mom, catching up on life in general. Trent and Teresa spin at the center of the room, having their first dance. Michi sits in a corner, nursing a tall drink.

I think she could use someone to talk to.

I cross the room, politely pushing my way through thick crowds of people, until I finally reach Michi. She takes a sip from her glass, which smells like it contains the world's most potent margarita.

"Great party, huh?" She looks drunk already.

"Yeah, it's a blast." I sit down next to my best friend. "Are you missing him?"

"What the hell do you think?" she slurs. "Here there's a wedding going on, and all the couples around, and your folks, and my folks, and you and

William … and here I am with a goddamn drink as my company and that's it!" She emphasizes her point by hovering the gauntleted hand over the glass. Sparks appear around it, then it's full again.

"You're drunk, Michi."

"You're drunk right I'm damn," she stumbles. She gets a little weepy. "I miss Fahaian … he should be here now, we should be together …"

She leans her head on my shoulder. I brush her hair gently away from her face. "It's all right. He promised you he'd be back. King's promise, remember?"

Her eyes are clearly showing her intoxication, they aren't even both looking in the same direction. "Well, what good does *that* do me right *now?* I got no boyfriend, everybody else is getting action …" She falls over on me. "Jeezus, my balance sucks ass tonight."

I chuckle softly. "You're drunk, Michi. It does things to your balance."

She takes another swig of the margarita. "How d'you know? I never seen you drink in m'life!"

"Because I don't like to drink, that's why." I put an arm around Michi's shoulders, as she continues to slump against me. "Listen, don't get too down about it. Fahaian promised to be back. I trust him, don't you?"

She whimpers slightly in my embrace. Finally she relents. "Yeah, I guess …"

"So trust him. He'll be back, he said he would be. He's bringing help. He's probably helping us out right now." I hug her tightly. "The next wedding we'll be going to is gonna be yours, Michi, I promise."

She smiles very drunkenly, beaming at me with half-opened eyes. "Thanks, Alanna." Her stomach rumbles. She stands up and wobbles slightly. "If you'll excuse me, I hafta go puke now." She tries to make her way quickly through the crowd, but it's difficult when she's stumbling all over the place. I don't want to laugh, but I can't help it.

William makes his way back over to my side. "Is she missing him?"

I nod. "She started off missing him, but in about fifteen minutes she'll be missing her lunch, too." I look up at my fiancé. "What about you, how do you feel?"

He wraps his arm around me. "Scared, actually."

My mood turns instantly. "What are you scared of?"

"I imagine the same thing you're scared of. Death. Dying. Seeing all my friends die around me." He clutches me tighter. "Losing you."

I lean into his chest, my own arms around him. "I can understand that, I fear the same things." Our eyes meet. "I want to say, though, that my existence is whole because you're in my life."

His eyes, which were starting to darken again, come back from the brink. "Really? I'm glad for that, because my life is complete with you, too." He brings his hand down to mine, to touch the ring again. "I want you to know, before any battle happens … that no matter what I want to spend eternity with you."

My heart leaps into my throat. It's pounding so hard I'm surprised he can't hear it. I wrap both of my hands around his and start leading him out of the party.

We make our way down the darkened hallway, toward my room. Just outside the door, I pull William into a tight embrace, yanking myself up to wrap my arms around his neck. Our lips meet in the darkness … desperate, hungry. Our bodies are acting on their own volition, on an impulse we've fought for so long but is finding its purpose in being tonight.

We could die tomorrow.

He carries me into the room, never once letting go of our kiss. Our hands roam freely, exploring each other's secrets. My heart continues its desperate, passionate rhythm. Clothes begin flying off of our bodies. We stagger our way over to the bed, our clinch only growing more needy. William's lips move to places I've never known could feel so incredible. Our desire is unstoppable. I feel his presence deeply within my being, overwhelming, folding me into one existence with this man I love so dearly.

The momentum is building.

I'm atop him, writhing, our love the only thing keeping me sane. He clutches me, holding me tight to him, moving with me. My pulse speeds up beyond anything I've ever experienced. At the last moment, when everything reaches its peak and a deep, passionate warmth washes over my body, I let out a yelp and my wings unfurl out of reflex, dipping and rising with my quick, panting breaths.

God, I just want to spend forever here, like this.

My strength falters, and I collapse down on top of William, still joined with him, both of us desperate to catch our breath. Our eyes meet in the darkness. In his eyes is a light that I've never seen before ... the total opposite of the darkness in them when we first met long ago.

He knows joy now, as I do as well.

My hand traces around his face, touching him gently, along his facial features, his scar, his hair. My fingers want to remember his face like this, forever. I feel the heat of his body against mine, the sweat cooling on our skin.

He lifts his head and kisses me gently, lovingly. "This moment is perfect." He wraps his arms around me.

"I agree." I smile up at him. "Stay with me tonight, William. Tonight and every night, until the end of the world and beyond."

He takes a deep, shuddering breath, and smiles back at me. "I promise, Alanna. I will."

I slide down off of him, and we cuddle close and tight to each other, lying beneath the blankets of my bed, until sleep finally overtakes us. My last thought as I slip into slumber stays with the positive.

We're going to win. This love is too perfect to lose.

August 27th

I'm reluctant to get out of bed this morning, knowing what's coming, and knowing what I'm leaving behind. The prone form of William, my beloved, my fiancé, is keeping me warm and safe right now. Why should I leave this?

Because every supernatural on the planet is depending on you, my mind responds. *Now get up and take your responsibility!*

I sit up and stretch my spine, which is surprised when a hand gently rubs up and down it. I look over and see that William is awake as well. He's smiling widely up at me.

"Heck of a night, wasn't it?"

I playfully slap his thigh. "You know it, mister." I turn and lay down next to him one more time, to kiss him deeply. "There'll be more where that came from afterward, I promise."

We both smile at each other. *This is probably going to be our last moment of enjoyment for some time, so we'd better make the most of it.*

Once we're out of bed and dressed, we make our way hand-in-hand to the living room. To my surprise, Dad intercepts us in the hallway. He doesn't say a word at first, simply looking the two of us over.

When it seems obvious that this silent treatment is making William squirm, Dad finally relents and smiles. "Why don't you go on ahead, William? I need to talk to Alanna for a minute." He motions for me to follow him into his and Mom's room.

"It's okay, Alanna, I'll meet you there." William kisses me and keeps walking down the hallway. Dad motions again, and I follow him into the room.

To my surprise, there's no comment about me and William coming out of my room together, no suspicions voiced about what we were doing. Instead, it's just me and Dad alone in his room, where he's rummaging through a chest of drawers next to the bed.

"Dad?" I helpfuly chime.

He looks up and smiles. "Sit down, Alanna. We need to have a talk ... don't worry, it's nothing too bad."

My heart is thrumming hard, but I sit down on the bed next to Dad. Evidently he finally finds what he's looking for, as he turns back toward me, something enclosed in his hand.

"Things are going to get very dangerous soon, so I have something I need to tell you, and to give to you." Dad motions toward his closed hand. "Let me give this to you first. It's something I've kept for a long time, and it's only right you should have it."

Dad takes one of my hands in his free one, and lays the item in his closed hand into my palm. My fingers close around the item … it's cold and metallic, and heavy. When Dad moves his hand, I find that he's given me a large, military-style tactical watch with a metal band.

"What is this?"

He smiles. "This watch is a modern Sharpe heirloom. I received it from my father … your grandfather Kenneth, whose grave we visited. He got it from *his* father, your great-grandfather, as an inheritance after he died in World War II."

I raise an eyebrow. "I thought the World War II Guardsman gave the Sword to my grandfather."

"He did, actually. Dad's father wasn't the Guardsman, the Sword belonged to his uncle Jefferson, but Jefferson never had any descendants … he was gay, you see … so he tapped my dad as the new Swordbearer once he left the Army."

I nod solemnly. "Thanks, Dad."

Dad pulls me into his arms. "There's one other thing I want to tell you, Alanna. In the short time you've held the Sword, that you've been the Guardswoman, I can easily see that you've done many, many great things with the power."

My eyes are warming up.

"Among those great things, you rescued both myself and your mother. For this, there's no amount of thanks that would ever be enough. I just want to let you know, before it's too late …" He strokes my hair and kisses my forehead gently. "… that I'm extremely

175

proud of you, and that in my eyes, you have surpassed me as the Guardsman. I trust the future of the world to no one more than I do to you."

I clutch Dad tightly. So much of my existence in the last few years has been dedicated to finding this man, to bringing him home, to returning his soul to him … I'm only now realizing the exact breadth and depth of how much I missed having him in my life. "Thank you, Daddy."

Dad kisses the top of my head. "Oh no, Alanna. Thank *you*." He squeezes me gently one last time, then stands up and leaves the room. I stand up to follow, but as I walk out toward the hallway I hook the watch through the belt of the Sword's scabbard. I will carry both of my family's symbols … the ancient one and the modern one … into this final battle.

When I get into the dining room, Aunt Kitty and Uncle Cyrus are already there, along with Mom and Dad. They wave us over to them.

"Guys, here's the plan," Uncle Cyrus intones. "This morning, I'm moving the Ranch to the forecast location outside of Boise. That's when the Attack division's going to make their move. Michika's mages will set up a perimeter shield, which should prevent any SSA troops from entering but won't stop any powers from escaping, all the better for us."

Dad clears his throat. "While this is going on, Alanna, you and I will be standing at the door of the Ranch house. If any agents come through the shield, it'll be up to us to stop them."

"Non-lethal whenever possible," I insist. "The rank-and-file SSA agents are only doing their jobs they're forced to do, so there's no need for excessive bloodshed."

Dad nods. "As you wish, Alanna." I can tell he's clearly not happy, and that's the military man in him, but that's the only way I know how to fight this war.

"Where is Michi, anyway?" I ask.

Aunt Kitty points her thumb behind her. I look over her shoulder and see Michi, lying on a nearby couch, an ice pack on her head. Every so often she moans.

"Michika had a little too much to drink last night, and now she's paying the price," Uncle Cyrus intones.

"She got shitfaced," Aunt Kitty confirms.

Poor girl. "Is she going to be in any shape to fight?"

"She will," Uncle Cyrus confirms. "Give me about an hour with her and she'll be fighting fit."

"All right," I respond. "William, I'll need you to set up your field hospital as soon as possible. I don't doubt we're going to see a lot of casualties probably within the first hour."

William nods and squeezes my hand. "You can count on me."

"Excellent," Uncle Cyrus responds. "We'll get this show on the road in about three hours. Everyone get whatever you want kept nailed down around the house in preparation for the spell."

Uncle Cyrus and Aunt Kitty stand up and attend to business … Aunt Kitty around the room, Uncle Cyrus with Michi … leaving me with Mom, Dad, and William.

"This is it," I try to start conversation with.

"Yeah," Dad mutters. "I just hope that we're ready for what Gabe wants us to do."

I take a deep breath. "So do I, believe me." I turn to Mom. "Will you be able to fight with us?"

She nods serenely. "Alanna, I've been held against my will for three years by the regime we are going to fight today. You can count on me to give it all I've got."

I'm happy to hear that. Impulsively, I go over to my parents and hug them both tightly. "Both of you stay safe, okay?"

They don't respond, they simply continue to hug me. They can't promise me they'll be safe, not when this is what they did as a living long ago. They know what to expect, and one of those expectations is that danger to life and limb is just another part of the job.

The next three hours are spent gathering our troops, getting them to their positions, securing all the loose items within the Ranch house, and speeding up Michi's recovery from her hangover. The time moves almost too quickly. Before I'm aware of it, Uncle Cyrus is calling for everyone to come in the house.

"Folks, this is it. Hang on to something!" Uncle Cyrus clutches a wall and closes his eyes, focusing the spell around him and the land we stand on. One hand clutches a table that's been bolted to the floor. The other one grabs on William and refuses to let go.

The floor lurches underneath us, as the Ranch lifts off of the ground, leaving Alberta behind. I remember the feeling of this spell, that it feels like a rocket taking off. I clutch to William tightly, looking over to him.

God, if You can only keep one person safe and alive in this conflict, let it be this man!

Just as suddenly as it lifted off, the Ranch begins a descent. With a shuddering thud, we finally reach the ground. We all look around at each other.

"Everyone safe?" I call out.

Several responses around the room confirm that everyone came through alive and well. My moment of relief is broken, however, when gunfire erupts outside the Ranch house.

"THIS IS THE SUPERNATURAL SUPPRESSION AGENCY! YOU HAVE ONE MINUTE TO SURRENDER! AFTER THAT, WE WILL ATTACK!"

Oh no …

I rush over to one of the windows, looking toward the Ranch fence. What greets my eyes is a thick, pulsating line of blueshirts, several of which with weapons drawn and pointed toward the house. My heart begins to drop as the realization sets in.

We were never going to ambush them. They're ambushing us!.

Maelstrom

Chapter Seventeen: Trapped

August 27th, continued

I quickly motion to Michi. "Shields up, now!"

Michi nods, turning toward a line of mages nearby. "Okay guys, like I taught you. Together in unison!" The mages raise their hands, joining them together and chanting.

I turn to the rest of the group. "Outside, Attack division! Be ready to fight as soon as you get out the door."

Both of the front doors open wide as the Attack division storms outside. Unfortunately, our grace period expires early when they do, and gunfire erupts. I hear at least one of my forces fall.

Keep it together, girl. I motion toward Dad. "With me, at the door, now!"

Dad nods, drawing the Sabre and allowing the Penitent to be free once more. I draw my own Sword, loosing the Guardswoman and standing by the door, waiting for any altercation. I'm conscious of William behind me, calling out to the Support teams and sending out field medics, who rush past mine and Dad's position.

The first blueshirt appears, one who apparently was inside the shield when it went up. He has a basic military rifle, and is trying to shoot Dad. Dad responds by throwing the blueshirt off of his feet and pinning him down with the Sabre. I reach down and grasp the man by his shirt, throwing him back off of the porch,

183

where Teresa Gracin hits him with an ice blast and freezes him in place.

I'm satisfied with this non-lethal confrontation, until more gunfire rings out, shattering the ice statue and killing the blueshirt within.

They don't give a damn about their own troops!

I try to keep myself under control and not rush headlong into the battle, but it's already starting to take its toll on our forces. I witness numerous supernaturals going down with gunshot wounds, only to be pulled out of the line of fire by our field medics. William has them well-trained. Four more blueshirts find their way to the porch, where me and Dad easily repel them. Not everybody can adhere to the non-lethal mandate, though, as I watch Aunt Kitty gun down a blueshirt who gets too close to Michi.

Our first-day casualties are manageable, but still tough to get a grasp on. Three are dead already. Another twenty-six are injured. Among the dead, to my regret, is Samuel Urich, who caught a stray round to the head while tending to an injured supernatural. It's a shame, really, I didn't really hate him, he was just a bit of a jerk.

Our best informant right now on the enemy is the television, and tonight I'm with William watching the news reports. An anchorman comes on the screen after a "Special Report" picture disappears.

"Good evening, we've received word here at the network that Alanna Sharpe's terror network is on the ropes. The terror mastermind's compound was located by the SSA this morning on the outskirts of Boise, next to the border between Idaho and Oregon. Several teams of SSA agents are now circling the compound, and an initial siege resulted in an enemy loss of over half of their force. This did not come without any cost, however, the SSA is reporting that twelve agents were injured, but no fatalities as the SSA is a professionally-trained law enforcement force."

"What a load of crap!" Michi roars as she enters the room. "We saw the one buy it outside the door!"

"They're trying to spin it so that it sounds like they're winning," William explains. I shush both of my friends so that I can hear the report.

"… word this evening that President Jennifer Regent is expected to meet with the SSA force's commanders, to congratulate them on a job well done. President Regent's popularity has skyrocketed since her husband's murder, also at the hands of the terrorist Alanna Sharpe, and public opinion for supernatural rights is at an all-time low thanks to recent events and the efforts of the SSA."

The report makes me angrier the more I hear, but one thing sticks out with me. *Jennifer's coming here?*

I look over at my friends, with a pang of regret. An idea is starting to form in my mind, but it's not one they're going to like.

"What do you think, Alanna?" William's voice interrupts my thoughts.

My face darkens. "I think it's a long fight ahead, guys, and that we'll need to fight tooth and nail."

"I agree," Michi chirps. "I'm going to meet with the mages and set up a couple of attack parties."

We both nod toward Michi, who makes her way out of the room. William stands up and reaches his hand out to me. "Are you coming?"

I nod gently. "In a little bit. I've got some thinking to do."

He smiles and nods. "Don't think for too long." He walks out into the dining room.

The darkness of the TV room matches my mood. I saw the size of the forces out there. We're outnumbered nearly 20-to-1. For every casualty we take, they can afford to take so many more. It's looking more and more hopeless, the more I think about it.

A traditional fight is not going to win this war. Traditional fighting will only get us exterminated. We need another plan …

I sigh deeply. I have a plan, but it means that I have to betray a lot of trust. *I don't want to do it, but …*

Gabe walks into the room, almost like he sensed what I'm thinking. "What's on your mind, Alanna?"

His voice startles me: it sounds so cold tonight. "I don't think we're going to do any good trying to hit the SSA face to face. We need a different strategy."

Gabe sits down next to me. "I'd be inclined to agree, especially after today. What do you propose?"

I motion to the TV. "The report tonight said that Jennifer Regent's going to make an inspection of the troops sieging us. That might be an opportunity, if one of us can get behind enemy lines."

Gabe strokes his chin. "Very true. Who do you propose should go?"

I take a deep breath, looking toward the agent. "You need to promise me that no one will know about this, okay?"

He looks confused. "Who are you sending?"

I tap my chest with my palm, then turn and leave the TV room. Gabe's well-versed in half-truths, so covering me shouldn't be a problem for him. I use the darkness to my advantage, spreading my wings and taking off into the nighttime. Once airborne, I can see the extent of the enemy's assembly, and realize that counting their numbers is going to be pointless: there's far too many, much more than the 20 troops' worth of fighters the dossier calls for.

Was the dossier a setup? I thought it was a little too easy to get around DC …

I start concentrating on finding a command center, some place where I can get inside. I have two ways I can do this. I can go peacefully, and convince them to let me in, or I can go in afire, fighting all the way.

Let's try the peaceful way first.

I bank into a slow downward spiral, at a clearing close to the entrance of the command center. Like I expected, I'm immediately spotted by SSA agents close to the building, who rush over to meet me, guns drawn.

I touch down and immediately collapse my wings and raise my hands. "Don't shoot. I want to negotiate a settlement!"

The agents look confused. One of them, clearly a commander or sergeant or something, approaches me carefully. "What kind of supernatural asks to negotiate? Your kind is all killers!"

Great, your ignorance is going to make this difficult. "I'm the main one you're after. Take me and leave the others alone. No more blood needs to be shed here."

The commander, in his 30's, runs his eyes up and down me, suddenly spotting the Sword. His face goes pale. "Oh my God, this is Alanna Sharpe!" He raises his rifle, keeping the muzzle end pointed at my left eye. "Search her! Disarm her!"

The other three agents approach me, frisking me a little too closely for comfort. One of them unbuckles the scabbard of the Sword from around my waist. When another one tries to draw the Sword, it shocks them.

"What the hell?" He grabs the front of my shirt. "What do you have hooked up to this thing? Disarm it now!"

"I can't."

"Don't give me that, bitch!" He knocks me down to the ground.

Don't fight back. You need to get inside.

"I'm serious, I can't disarm it. There's nothing *to* disarm, I'm the only one who's allowed to draw it."

The blueshirt tosses it over to his commander, who is careful to grab the Sword by the leather of the scabbard. "Very well. Inside, supernatural."

I stand up, placing my hands behind my head. Another blueshirt pokes me in the back with his weapon, forcing me to walk forward. I wind up following the commander inside the building, which is illuminated inside by intense fluorescent lighting. It almost hurts my eyes, it's so bright. My hands are secured behind my back with what feels like a nylon restraint, and I'm grabbed roughly by the arm and forced to march down a long hallway, equally as bright as the entryway.

I look to either side of me at the blueshirts holding me captive. Both of them barely look older than me. One even has freckles on his face and a sad expression. "What's wrong?" I ask him.

His expression turns instantly to anger. "Shut your hole, supernatural!" He squeezes my arm roughly. "No talking."

They continue to push me forward, toward another room that's nowhere near as brightly lit. The commander, who's walked in front of us the whole way, brings us to a halt with a hand signal.

"Wait here." He opens the door to the new room and goes inside. I can't hear whatever conversation goes on, but about a minute later he opens the door again. "She's ready. Bring her inside."

The other two blueshirts push me forward again, and I walk with them into the darkened room, apparently a war room of some sort, lined from floor to ceiling with video monitors. A lot of the scenes are unfamiliar places, but one stands out to me, a CCTV image of the front gates of the Ranch. I know it's current because I can even see the pulsation of the magic shield around the land.

"Right here, put her right here," the commander leads his charges. They move me to a particular place on the floor. The freckled blueshirt whips out a nightstick and knocks me behind the knees, forcing me to kneel.

Legs throbbing, shoulders pulled back in an unnatural position, I feel a foot pushing down on my upper back, forcing my face to the floor. My only awareness of my surroundings is now hearing others talk.

"That's good, thank you men." The commander clears his throat. "She claims to be coming to negotiate. She was only armed with this weapon, but it's armed with some sort of security device so we can't even pull it out."

"Understood, sergeant. That will be all." It's a female voice.

"Are you sure, ma'am? You do know who this is, right?"

"I am completely aware of my adversary. It's all right. Go rejoin your troop and wait for my signal."

I hear the sergeant's heels click. "As you wish, ma'am." He whistles, the signal for the other two blueshirts to leave. I'm now all alone with my interrogator.

"After all this time, I finally see you in person. You can color me honored."

The sarcasm drips off of her words. If there was any doubt in my mind as to who this is, it's gone now. I look up at my interrogator.

The grinning face of Jennifer Regent stares back at me, the Sword lying underneath her foot. To one side, another weapon leans against the seat she currently occupies, an almost comically long, two-handed broadsword.

My blood runs cold.

It's the Damnation Blade.

Chapter Eighteen: Duel

August 28th

The clock behind Jennifer crosses past midnight. She's still sitting there, just grinning at me. She taps her fingers on the arm of the chair, trying to bore holes through me with her eyes.

Those eyes … they show her mania. They're bloodshot, lined with so many bright red veins I could create a topographical map. The irises are nearly non-existent, and what I can see of them is bright green. Her breathing is starting to speed up considerably.

Her teeth grind. That's the most unnerving thing about this situation.

"Well?" she demands. "Aren't you going to say anything to your President?"

My eyes darken. "I don't recognize the authority of anyone whose policy is death to my kind. I'm here to offer a compromise."

Jennifer leans back in her chair. "I'm listening."

My own breathing is coming quicker. "I'm sure that neither one of us wants to see any further bloodshed on our respective sides, so I'll make an offer to end this struggle. You leave the Ranch and its inhabitants alone. Disassemble this insane force you've created, and let them go home to their families and their lives."

She strokes her chin. "What's in it for me?"

"Me, plain and simple. I'll give myself up to you, and face whatever you believe is justice for any and all crimes you've linked to me. You can do with me what you wish."

She lowers her eyelids and crosses her arms. "And if I refuse?"

I grit my teeth. "Then the Ranch will continue to fight, and eventually destroy your forces. Their blood will be on your hands."

She takes in a sharp breath through her teeth. It sounds like a snake hissing in warning. "See, that's the problem here, Alanna … may I call you Alanna? Anyway, the problem is I already have you, and as far as blood goes, the more the better!" She grins and stands up. "I don't care how much blood I have to draw to end your kind."

Oh well, it was a long shot anyway. "What kind of President are you, anyway? Your administration has done absolutely nothing but persecute supernaturals as long as you've been in power."

"Ah ah, as long as *Carleton* has been in power, we've tried to make life better for the human population. This is merely the culmination of that policy."

I strain against my restraints, but they feel like they're tightening with every motion. "You're insane. I saw your office."

"Did you, now?" She starts laughing. "I had a feeling you would. After all, why do you think I'm here?"

My heart starts to sink. "So it *was* a trap."

"Exactly." She comes face-to-face with me and jabs her finger into my chest. "And you fell right into it! I can't believe you let yourself get suckered so easily!" She laughs in my face.

Her breath smells familiar … like Scolar's, but …

"Yes, I made sure you had that dossier. I made sure you found poor, dearly departed Carleton's body, that

192

the White House guards saw you." She grins wider and more maniacally. "Who do you think kept the streets of Washington clear that day, huh?"

This is getting out of hand too quickly. *I've completely been caught in the spider web, and the black widow is about to consume me. What a foolish way to die.*

"There's just one question I have before I exterminate you and your kind like the roaches you are," she intones, moving ever closer to me until she's in my face again. "Where in the world did you hide General Scolar?"

This might be to my advantage ... she doesn't know he's dead ...

Wait, her breath, that smell ...

She reeks of the Inferno!

"He's in the Ranch, in a secure location. He'll be moved if anyone threatens. If you make any move on my forces, he'll be dead before you can even reach him."

She snorts. "You're bluffing."

"Am I? I've killed before. You made sure of that."

She laughs again, a sound I'm quickly getting sick of. "Oh, you mean that whole Chicago thing? Collateral damage, I needed you to be the villain I was creating. There's nothing the public loves more than a good villain to rail against."

I growl. "Damn you, it's *my life* you've been manipulating! What gives you that right?" I struggle harder against the restraints.

"Don't even think about it, Alanna." Her eyes narrow intensely and her mood switches from jovial to threatening in an instant. "After all, the support staff here doesn't take kindly to Guardsmen."

She motions toward three of the blueshirts manning the monitors around us. One of them turns around toward me, and his eyes are glowing a hellish red.

Demons. Her bodyguards are demons.

"Every one of these gentlemen was handpicked ... by me, of course ... to come to this place, to confront the Guardsman, to torment her, and to destroy her. You've saved us some time, of course, by carelessly making your way here, trying to confront me. What did you hope to accomplish?"

I need a new approach, fast. I take a deep breath before playing my next card. "I've spoken to Alastair. He regrets what you've become."

She stops short in her diatribe, looking toward me with a confused expression. "My dear brother? How have you spoken to him, he's been dead as long as you've been alive."

I smirk. "I have my ways, Jennifer ... may I call you Jennifer?" I sense I have her caught off-guard, and press my point. "He's in Hell right now, burning for eternity, cycling through every ring for each sin he committed here. He wants to spare you the same fate. If you destroy us, there's no way you'll avoid it."

She shoots me a blank look, then turns the tables and surprises me by acting very un-Presidential, spitting on the floor. "Why should I give a damn about what some piddling damned soul thinks? He really should know his place."

Well, that confirms my suspicions. "He's concerned about the soul of his sister ... Mamuna."

She growls, gritting her teeth. "So you know."

I grind my own teeth and grimace back a grin. "Yeah, princess. So what, you're trying to prove something by destroying all supernaturals?"

She roars back over to me and grabs my chin. "Greater than that, Sharpe! I can do greater things than Lucifer could have dreamed! I can deliver the entire living world to Hell, I can eliminate Eden!" She comes nose-to-nose with me. "I can destroy the Guardsman forever!" She throws me back down to the floor, pacing maniacally. "You haven't a single clue, Sharpe. You don't know what it's like in Hell, what it's like to be a woman there, to be taught for your entire damned eternal existence that you're inferior just because you're missing male equipment."

I snuffle harshly. "I might have some idea. So that's it, then? Trying to prove a point, some great women's liberation thing? Because let me tell you, us *actual* women don't really need help from the likes of *you*."

Mamuna reaches down and grabs me by the scruff of the neck. "Such a short-sighted little girl." Her eyes narrow. "This isn't about men versus women, Sharpe. This is about becoming even greater than Lucifer, about even outdoing the Lord of Lies himself!"

I wriggle out of her grip. "What about your father? Where does Mammon fit into this?"

She scoffs at my question. "What does it matter to you?"

"Call it morbid curiosity."

She laughs. "Very well. He's in this room." She pats the Damnation Blade.

Every time she reaches for that weapon, my heart drops. I can feel the heavy demonic presence now, fitting of a prince and princess of Hell. "In the Blade?"

195

She grins again. "After all, the full potential of this weapon cannot be reached unless a demon bonds with it. I bet you didn't know *that*, did you?"

I growl loudly. "That still doesn't explain one thing, though. Why did Carleton have to die?"

Mamuna lowers down in her chair. "*Some*body had to carry this thing. You poor, deluded fool." She pats my cheek. "Carleton Regent never existed before twenty years ago ... he's been a simulacrum, carrying the Blade for me until such time that it was time to strike." She laughs harshly. "The Blade's been hiding in plain sight the whole time, and you never knew until now."

Things are getting too dangerous. "So what do you mean by eliminate Eden?" I try to guide the conversation back toward getting a reveal of her plan.

"Exactly what it sounds like, hatchling." The use of that word makes my skin crawl ... I spent too long being called it by Scolar. "Haven't you learned, yet? Everything is connected. What you know as Avalon once went by a different name ..."

Things are starting to make some sense ... I can take a guess what she means. "The Garden of Eden?"

"Yes, precisely. You're such a good student!" She sounds too enthusiastic. "Haven't you wondered why no one has ever found it, even with all the searching? It's because as punishment for the original sin, God ensured the location of the Garden and its secrets would never be learned by *separating it into its own plane of existence!*"

I need to get out of these restraints, but they're too tight. "So you want to destroy Eden? Isn't that enough, do you have to take the supernaturals out at the same time?"

"I thought you knew, they're one and the same, little girl," Mamuna growls at me. "All supernaturals hold within them a sliver of Eden, a genetic reminder that the Garden once existed on Earth. Without that reminder, Earth is lost to Heaven … and thus becomes *mine!*" She storms over to the bank of monitors. "We've wasted enough time on this fruitless discussion. Commence Operation Glass Jaw. We end this now!"

The demon technicians tap away at their panels, leaving me at the center of the room, forced to watch helplessly. The banks of monitors other than the one looking at the Ranch start filling up with SSA troops, storming into streets, paths, fields, city squares.

Nothing happens.

Mamuna looks confused. She turns back to the techs. "Where the hell are the dragons?"

One of the demons looks up at Mamuna. *"The dragons never deployed. We can't get any signal out to the laboratory."*

"A minor setback. Send out the signal to our alternates."

The demon nods and turns back to his panel. On the screens, the SSA agents continue to look around, a little confused. Now the signals are being interspersed with international news feeds showing the bewildered blueshirts standing around, waiting.

Mamuna screams. "What now?!"

Another of the demons, looking fearful, turns toward the princess. *"No signal was received by the* alternates. It looks like they've already been met by someone else."

I start to laugh, quietly at first, then louder so that Mamuna can hear me. She turns around in a rage. "What's so damned funny, you little twerp?! What did you do?"

Now I have reason to really smile. "Glass Jaw is a failure, Mamuna. We destroyed your dragons in DC, and our allies around the world took care of your 'alternates.' You shouldn't have listed them in that dossier." I'm laughing hysterically now.

Mamuna's not pleased. She screams with a demon's roar. *"DAMN YOU!"* She yanks a gun out of the holster of one of the demons, pointing it toward me, her bloodshot eyes wide. "You've humiliated the New Empire! This plan was perfect, and you just *screwed* me!"

"Lady, you screwed yourse—"

My words are cut off by the barrel of the pistol being shoved into my mouth. She pulls back the hammer. Her voice becomes a whisper. "I can at least destroy the Guardsman. Say good night, bitch."

What's it going to be like to die? I guess I'll find out …

"Hold, Madam President." A sickeningly familiar voice cuts through the chaos. My heart pumps faster. There he comes, striding in the door, in his full regalia, like nothing had ever happened.

Scolar. How is this possible?! Am I already dead and having a flashback before my soul expires?

"General, how good of you to come." Mamuna takes the gun out of my mouth and backs away from

198

me. "This is Alanna Sharpe, the terrorist mastermind. Destroy her at once!"

Scolar nods. "As you wish." He turns his face down to me, narrowing his eyes. "It's a shame, really. Such a long rivalry, to end like this."

He reaches for the Sabre, the one I swear I destroyed two years ago. It's back to its old form, not the changed version Gabe made. He draws the weapon, and the Invader's armor closes around him. The Sabre is raised high above the hell knight's head, in an executioner's pose.

All of my nightmares are coming true at once.

My breathing quickens. *I'm dead. I'm really dead this time. Farewell, everyone …*

Wait, that's weird. Did he just wink at me?

The weapon cuts through the air, not toward my neck but toward the demons running the control panels. Two of them dissolve into dust in one stroke.

Now I'm confused.

That confusion doesn't last for long, once the Invader tears off a piece of his armor, near his wrist … a HoSIP. The camouflage falls instantly, revealing that the Invader is a fake, and the real knight is the Penitent.

Dad …

The Penitent rushes over to Mamuna's chair at the center of the room and kicks the Sword toward me. I turn around to catch it in my bound hands, then slide it out of the scabbard. The Guardswoman easily breaks the bonds and brings the Sword around to *en garde,* standing back to back with the Penitent.

Mamuna screams. "Attack, you fools!"

199

Another company of demons, four of them in total, rushes toward us. Combining our effort, me and Dad are able to make short work of them. We turn our attention back toward Mamuna, who grabs the Damnation Blade and runs out of the room. A heavy steel door closes behind her, preventing us from making chase.

Dad sheathes the Sabre. He's clearly not happy. "What the hell, Alanna? What were you trying to do?"

I sheathe the Sword, turning to face him. "I needed to find out what's going on! I got some good information, we just need to use it now to our advantage."

Dad groans. "Don't do this again, Alanna. You hear me?" He sounds irritated, but I can also hear his fear and concern. He came out of love, not out of anger.

I nod quietly. "I won't. I promise."

He rushes up to me and hugs me tightly. "We were so worried about you."

I pick up my arms and return the embrace, holding Daddy tight to me. "So was I for a while." We release the hug. "What now?"

"Well, thanks to this escapade, we're going to have to fight our way back to the Ranch. We already fought our way here, so ..."

"Who else is with you?"

"*The whole family!*" a familiar beastly voice screams. William, grown into the wendigo, bursts into the room. He begins shrinking back into himself as he continues to talk. "*Ariel has the* guards on the run, but we need to go now!"

"Right. All of us." Dad motions to me. "Come on, Alanna, let's go."

I unfurl my wings. "I have a faster way." My face turns up toward the ceiling, spewing a firecast through the metal and creating a hole to the midnight sky. I grab Dad and William, growing into my dragon form, and flap my way up through the hole just like I learned to launch from flying with Mom.

Jump and hard flap …

Once airborne, I glide over to where another familiar dragon blasts the ground with fire, holding the soldiers back. Mom looks over toward me, then starts flapping faster once she knows I'm right behind her. While flying over the troops, we continue to strafe them, keeping everyone on the run. Blueshirts scatter left and right, trying to get away from the fire we're spreading.

We accelerate once the Ranch is within spitting distance, punching our way through the magic shield to alight and land in the fields behind the Ranch house. The landing's a little rough, and I wind up rolling in the grass, but I scramble back to my feet and drop Dad and William before shrinking back into my human form.

Gabe is at the back door, waiting for us. "What's going on?" he demands.

I'm out of breath, but I rush up to him. "It's Mamuna … she's got the Blade … coming for Avalon … file was a trap …"

"I had a feeling about that." Gabe leads us all inside. "We need to prepare to defend the Avalon door. She's not going to hesitate after the first part of Glass Jaw failed."

I look up at Gabe at this information. "How did you …?"

"It's all over the news." He leads me into the TV room, where Michi is sitting, grinning and bouncing.

She runs up to me and hugs me tightly. "Fahaian came through! I knew he would!" She pulls me down to a seat while a news broadcast displays on the TV.

"... the United Nations is calling for a special meeting to discuss sanctions against the New Empire of America for unauthorized intervention into other member nations. In the meantime, no sources were available at either the SSA or the White House to confirm or deny the reports. Once again, a number of international news agencies are reporting that large numbers of Supernatural Suppression Agency troops have been sighted in capitals around the world, with apparently no purpose other than as a show of strength by the New Empire. The soldiers appeared to be looking for some kind of fight, as they were armed and ready for action, but no supernatural opponent was present."

A cheer rises from the main area, as the news circulates. *We've disrupted the first part of Glass Jaw. Now we need to stop the other two phases.*

The cheers are interrupted by the ground shaking. Not a natural earthquake either, this one feels decidedly demonic. All of us inside the house rush outside to see what the commotion is. What greets us is a stunning turn of events.

There's a tank outside. It's just fired a shell approaching the shield ... now it's moving through the shield ...

It lands in the middle of the Ranch house and explodes.

Chapter Nineteen:
Cataclysm

August 28th, continued

My ears are ringing. I can barely stand up. Smoke is saturating the air around us.

Mom! Dad! Michi! William!

I want to scream, but I don't know if I'm making any sound. I stagger toward the damaged area of the house, the foyer completely destroyed by the attack. I see motion, albeit labored motion. My eyes adjust through the haze and I spot a recognizable shape. Without thinking, I rush over toward it.

I get closer and realize that it's Aunt Kitty. Unfortunately, she's been pinned under rubble, and Uncle Cyrus is trying to pull her free. I rush over, wings unfurled, and try to help, lifting a timber off of her legs. Once it's lifted about three inches, Aunt Kitty drags herself out, groaning at the strain of the effort. Uncle Cyrus rushes around me to his wife's side, already powering a spell over her crushed thighs. He's saying something to me, but I can't understand it. I merely stagger away, looking for more people to help.

Teresa Gracin staggers toward me, in tears, soot coating her head-to-foot. Her left arm's shorter … the hand's been ripped off of it. I look toward where she just came from and see Trent, also pinned under rubble, except he's not coming back from this injury since a timber landed on his head. His powers did nothing to help him.

I clutch Teresa close to me. "We'll get you some help."

She nods and keeps weeping, and she's saying something or wailing, but I still can't hear her. I lead her through the chaos, even as medics start rushing through looking for survivors. William rushes over and takes Teresa from me, leading her away from the danger zone. I can see on the other side of the chasm the attack created that the medical station William and Grandmother built during the month's lull has been half-blasted to oblivion. Grandmother and Julian are scrambling around within, tending to every injured person that comes to them.

Another temblor shakes the ground, nearly knocking everyone off of their feet again. I turn around and see that the tank has fired another round. This one, however, has no shield to slow it down, so it's screaming at us at full steam. Just as it reaches its apex, though, it explodes in mid-air, creating another quake.

Directly in front of me, Michi has her gauntleted hand up, the last residue of a spell circling her hand. She intercepted it, stopped it from creating more damage.

The ringing's starting to go down. I'm panicking, looking around me. "Mom! Dad!"

"Over here!" Through the din I can hear Mom's voice, calling me back over near where we were when the shell struck. I flap my wings and lift off, zooming quickly across the chasm, and rejoin their side.

"Damn it, what the hell are they thinking?" Dad screams.

"They don't care, Dad. Mamuna made that clear, the more innocent blood the better as far as she's concerned." I clutch both my parents close to me. "We need to regroup!"

Another round shakes the ground. Michi is able to intercept this one as well, but both me and Dad look at each other meaningfully. "Are you thinking what I'm thinking?" he ponders.

"I think so." I draw the Sword, turning around and rushing the tank. Dad's shortly behind me, the Penitent waving his Sabre high. About twenty blueshirts rush to try to intercept us, grabbing at us, grabbing at our weapons, and they manage to slow us down enough to allow the tank to fire off another shot.

I look back toward Michi. She's clearly weakening … despite the edge being Durga's servant gives her, too much exertion's still going to leave her vulnerable. *We need to kill this thing now!*

I spin with the Sword stretched out, knocking aside several of the blueshirts trying to hold me back. There's a clear path between myself and the tank. I swing the Sword hard toward its armored belly.

The weapon recoils and nearly knocks me off of my feet. I swing away again. It repels me again. *I'm not even creating a dent!*

Dad joins me and together we hack away, but neither of our weapons is creating any damage: they're bouncing off like they're rubber swords. Maybe we're attacking the wrong part of the tank … I unfurl my wings and flap my way up to the top, near the turret. I can hear inside the machine that they're loading another round and preparing to fire again.

I raise the Sword high above my head, bringing it down on the barrel of the turret. The metal doesn't chink, but it dents. I hit it again and again and again, and my efforts are rewarded by creating a large kink in the weapon. Apparently the crew inside the tank hasn't been able to hear me hacking away, and I hear a "fire" command.

Probably a good time to get off this thing. I flap my wings and lift off, up and away from the machine, but my flight is too slow. The turret fires, but the kink in the barrel causes a misfire and blows the turret clean off of the machine. Right into me.

My flight path is disrupted, and I crash down to the ground, dropping the Sword. My chest hurts a lot, almost as bad as when I got picked up in the Inferno by Geryon. Thank God the turret didn't land on me, or else I really would have been dead, armored or not. I feel cautiously around my ribs, and I think I can feel a gap that isn't supposed to be there. I cough and taste blood.

No time. Have to get back to the Ranch house!

I scramble back to my feet, ribs screaming, and grab the Sword. The Guardswoman's armor closes around me, but doesn't minimize the pain at all. My eyes wince as my wings unfurl and I flap my way away from the smoldering hulk of the destroyed tank. The Penitent keeps pace with me, running underneath me, fighting back through the blueshirts that had been escorting the tank. We just barely reach the inside of the fence line before my strength gives out and I crash to the ground again. This time, though, I sheathe the Sword, then immediately grab my ribs once more.

Dad sheathes the Sabre and runs up to my side. "That should slow them down for a while, at least. They can't lob any more firebombs at us."

My teeth grind. "Yeah, but look around, Dad, how long can we hold out?" I motion toward the wrecked house. Michi's being helped by her own dad, while three medics are carefully moving Aunt Kitty onto a stretcher to carry her back to Grandmother. Mom's with William, trying to find more survivors of the blast, while some of the mages are frantically working together to re-establish the shield around the Ranch land. They're trying their best, but we're in disarray right now.

If Mamuna makes her move, we're doomed.

My eyes focus through the damage to the house, toward the Avalon door. There's two supernaturals guarding it right now, but only one of them has an attack power: Ian Raynor, the caustic gas-shooting man. The other one, conscripted into guarding the door, is Jerry Tile, who's holding what looks like the biggest rifle Aunt Kitty could spare from her arsenal.

Dad gently puts his hand on the one that's holding my ribs, and I wince in pain. "Go get treated, Alanna, you need it."

"I'm staying here!"

"Alanna, go! Your mom and I can handle being the front line for the time it takes you to get bandaged up!" He nearly pushes me away from him. Thinking better than to use my wings to fly over, I walk over to the medical area, where William is the first to greet me. He leads me away from the others, into Uncle Cyrus's workshop. Once I'm sitting on the workbench with my shirt hiked up, he starts wrapping me in gauze.

Every once in a while I wince when he hits the broken ribs.

"Sorry, Alanna. We need to make sure it's not going to shift and puncture a lung."

My voice is a little whimpery. "I can understand that, it just doesn't change the fact that it hurts." I wince again.

"We're running out of time, aren't we?"

I look over at my fiancé, at the sad expression on his face. I gently reach out a hand to stroke his face. "We just need to regroup and get ready for the next wave, that's all."

He shakes his head. He's getting depressed, or he's being realistic. "This was a hopeless task, right from the moment we took it on ourselves."

I pull his face up so that I can see it. "None of that, William. We're going to make it. We're going to survive, and win."

He sighs deeply. "I just wonder, though. There were things Gabe said about you while you were away, in the Inferno, and they've been sticking with me."

Now my attention's drawn away from the battle for the first time. "What kinds of things?"

He sighs. "A lot of it was attempts to keep our faith in you, to keep us believing you were coming back. This was especially when it looked like you'd never come back. But in one of those conversations, Gabe made mention of you being the 'ultimate Guardsman.'" He looks up, darkness in his eyes. "I think 'ultimate' in this case means 'last.'"

My stomach drops. *Does that mean all those damned souls in Hell were right? That this ends in nothing but death and pain for us all?* I pull my shirt back down and clutch to William's neck tightly. "Don't lose your hope, William, no matter what you do."

He returns the hug, gently so as not to hurt my ribs any further. "But it's so hard, Alanna … it's so damn hard …"

"I know it is, but I believed in us. I believed in our ability to overcome any obstacle, and that was what got me through the Inferno above and beyond focusing on Dad. It was you, William. You, Michi, Fahaian, all of us. Together, our power is unbeatable." I pull his face down to mine and kiss him gently. "This belief is real, this is true, and this is why we're going to win."

I manage to get a slight smile out of William. "You'd better get back to the front."

"Thanks. I love you too." I smirk playfully at him, leaving one last kiss on his lips before running back out of the workshop. My ribs already feel a little less painful.

Mom and Dad have been joined by Michi, who's frantically gnawing on an energy bar. Mom motions for me to join the group, and we all watch across the battlefield, watching the New Empire forces massing.

"They're getting ready to storm the place," Dad mutters.

"How are the mages doing?" Michi weakly asks.

"They've just barely got the shield up," Mom responds. "Other than that, it's going to be all us."

I look behind us and see that a skeleton crew of Attack division forces have joined us. One of them, surprisingly, is Teresa Gracin, wiping her merciless-expression eyes with a bandaged stub where her hand used to be. I turn back around to look out.

"All right, then let's meet them with a show of strength. Mom, care to do the honors?"

Mom nods, seemingly knowing what I'm asking her for. She closes her eyes and grows back into the dragon form, her body just barely avoiding falling into the crater caused by the tank attack. The blueshirts raise their weapons toward us. Mom responds by opening her maw and blasting a firecast toward the blue line. To our surprise, out from the fire column pours twelve lines of soldiers, in full battle uniforms, rushing the blueshirts. Michi shrieks loudly and happily, a sound which gets louder and happier when the force's commander makes his presence known.

"FAHAIAN!!!!"

The king looks over toward us and smiles widely. "I apologize for being late! Have we missed anything?"

Michi rushes out to where he stands and leaps happily into his arms. The battle continues to rage as the Jordanian troops start cutting easily through the lines of blueshirts; it's what you'd expect when a professionally-trained army confronts what amounts to a gang of street thugs. Our forces let out a whoop and start rushing in right behind the Jordanians. The blueshirts are shrinking backward, unable to handle the sheer strength they've been met with.

Another earthquake strikes, shifting our footing. *Oh no, not another tank …*

Dad's eyes narrow. His gaze is focused squarely on the horizon, toward the general direction of Mamuna's field headquarters. "What the hell is *that?*"

We all focus on where he's looking. A shadowy figure is rising head and shoulders above the

210

blueshirts, with giant proportions. It also looks vaguely … feminine?

I know who this is before I can even see her clearly. I don't even flinch when the realization hits me, since it was expected from the start.

Mamuna.

Chapter Twenty: Ragnarok

August 28th, continued

The sun is dropping behind the horizon, but the shadow looms over us still, the dark presence approaching. Mom and Dad get closer to each other, almost defensively, not wanting to leave each other's side. Right now I don't blame them one bit.

I wish William was here right now, instead of back with the injured.

My hand is in a death grip on the Sword, as the giant demon Mamuna approaches us. As she gets closer, we can see her more clearly than when she was simply a shadow on the horizon. She's fifty feet tall, at least, a vaguely feminine shape, coated with lizard's skin with green matted hair. Her eyes glow a hellish orange toward us, her tongue flits in and out of her mouth from time to time like a snake's. She grins toward us, reptilian teeth creating a sawtoothed smile.

"I should have known not to rely on humans to do a demon's job!" Her voice booms through the air, causing the Ranch house to shake on what's left of its foundations. My eyes travel down to her hip, where a belt and a scabbard hang.

She's carrying the Damnation Blade with her.

Mom and Dad look toward me, Mom still in her dragon form. Her dragon eyes are level with mine.

"Stay here and defend the door, Alanna. We're counting on you and the Guardswoman."

"And no matter what happens, remember that we both love you dearly."

Dad puts a gentle kiss on my forehead to emphasize the point. Mom blows smoke out of her nostrils.

My eyes are watering up. "I love you too."

Dad draws the Sabre, and the armor of the Penitent closes around him, obscuring his face. He turns around and places a hand gently on Mom's flank. She scoops the knight up in one of her forelegs, putting him up on her shoulders. She stands up on her haunches, lifts her wings, and launches herself into the dusky sky.

Michi and Fahaian rush over to where I'm standing. "Alanna, you okay?" Michi asks.

I can only point up in the sky, to where Mom and Dad are shrinking away from me, heading toward danger. A fire stream launches from Mom's mouth, hitting Mamuna square in the chest and pushing her backward. Her face shows mild discomfort, but she responds by swatting at the dragon. Mom flaps away slightly, trying to avoid another blow from the back of the demon's hand and sending another blast of flame, this time in the demon's face.

Mamuna screams and reaches for the Blade. My heart jumps. *No, not that!*

The Penitent leaps off of Mom's back, Sabre blade down, his body streaking toward Mamuna. The blade finds purchase in the demon's shoulder, causing her to scream. He gets up on his feet, yanking the Sabre out of the wound he's created and starts rushing up Mamuna's shoulder toward her head. Mamuna, however, grabs him and flings him down to the ground.

213

She reaches for the Damnation Blade. Her hand closes around its hilt. She pulls the weapon slowly out of its scabbard.

Mamuna grows even larger than she was, more muscular and even further demonic. Her hair becomes a flaming pyre. Her eyes narrow and glow even more brightly orange.

I'm panting. I can barely think. My stomach is tied up in knots.

This is how the world ends …

Mamuna lifts the Blade above her head, pointed downward, intending to run Dad through with it. Mom circles and hits the Blade with another firecast. The demon's unfazed, and turns with the weapon.

She hits Mom with it. I've never before heard the kind of shrill scream the dragon lets out, and I will never forget it as long as I have left on this planet. It's blood-curdling, and reverberates for what seems like miles. Before I can think, I'm growing into my own dragon, rushing out to grab Mom. She's falling like a rock, and I'm not sure if I'll reach her before she hits the ground.

My wings launch into their hard swimmer's stroke, pushing me through the air at breakneck speed. My forelegs reach out for the other dragon … stretching …

I catch her just before she hits the ground, banking to bring her down gently. Once she's down, she immediately begins shrinking into her human form. The wound never changes size, however; it remains as serious as it had been with the dragon, a long slash along her midsection.

It looks like it's starting to fester right before my eyes. I turn and bellow back toward the house. *"Michi, I need you! She's dying!"*

Michi launches herself out of the house and toward where we are. As she starts tending to Mom, I'm only able to watch as Mamuna brings the Blade down on Dad.

My scream finally draws the demon's attention. She grins down at me, that snakelike grin only made more demonic by the flaming head of hair. *"First we torment the Guardsman, we kill her allies and her family, and then we destroy her!"* Her tongue flicks in and out of her mouth again, and she continues her path toward the Ranch. I rush over to Dad's side, where he's sheathed the Sabre. Much the same as Mom, he has a slash wound across his midsection that's immediately festering. William this time rushes out of the house, coming to us.

"I'll do my best, Alanna. Go!"

I firecast toward Mamuna, but she barely notices it hitting her ankle. Impulsively, I grab the Sabre and fly back toward the house.

By this time, Mamuna is encountering the rest of our forces, trying to push her backward. The effort is valiant, but it's pointless, like a group of army ants trying to stop a foot from stepping on them. Teresa has the best chance of stopping her, forming ice walls at Mamuna's knee-level trying to slow her progress. She kicks them aside, while other supernaturals unfortunately meet the Blade, which does similar damage to what Mom and Dad are fighting to everyone it touches.

215

I know where she's headed. She's looking for the door.

I pump my wings faster, knocking into the backs of Mamuna's knees. The demon takes notice of me again and tries to hit me with the Blade, but I'm too fast for her slow swing. The blow instead takes out another huge chunk of the Ranch house. She turns and continues her trek toward the door, finally reaching it despite our forces' best efforts. Jerry Tile raises his weapon and fires full-auto into Mamuna's chest, only to be swatted aside by the Blade: I can clearly see his body flail as he's tossed back toward the Ranch house wreckage.

Mamuna's grin becomes even more maniacal. That snake tongue flickers faster. *"At last, Eden falls."* She reaches down for the knob of the door and opens it.

A lightning bolt greets her, knocking her backward. Six hands appear on the door jamb. A cheer erupts from the supernaturals as the owner of those hands comes out, standing nearly as tall as Mamuna does.

I'm happy to recognize the newcomer, too. *"Durga!"*

The goddess smiles over at us, then turns her attention to Mamuna. "I am sorry, my friend, but I cannot let you come through this door. I know the harm you intend on the other side."

Mamuna snarls. *"You are weak, goddess. You cannot stand against this kind of power."*

"We'll see." Durga assumes a combat stance, letting out all ten of her arms. Each one has a different weapon she intends to attack with. Her smile never fades. She's enjoying this a little too much, I think.

Mamuna raises the Damnation Blade and rushes Durga, who parries the Blade expertly to keep it from

216

crossing through the door. With a foot she closes the door, then spins around and jabs her dagger into Mamuna's side. The demon screams and turns again, swinging the Blade.

Durga ducks the swing, looping her chakram around the weapon and driving it down to the ground, which she follows up by pressing her sword against Mamuna's throat. "Stand down, demon, for you are as lost as your kinsman Mahishasura was."

Mamuna growls and knocks Durga back with a headbutt. *"I think not, fool!"* Mamuna brings the Blade upright once more, then back down. Durga meets the stroke with her bow, trying to hold the deadly weapon back.

Her strength is faltering …

The bow starts bending a little too much. It splits. The Blade passes between Durga's arms, landing on her shoulder. It continues through her body, only coming to a stop when it catches near the goddess's opposite hip.

Gabe's words about the Blade spring to mind, during this horrific spectacle. *It's the power of disbelief; once it wounds something with a large amount of belief behind it, disbelief takes over, and the injured party succumbs from this.*

Durga shrinks away from the blade, her wound grievous. Her breathing comes fast and heavy, labored as it is through the injury. She collapses right in front of the door, still trying to block Mamuna's path, even as she may well be dying. Despite her wounds and her weakened state she continues to fight, flinging her chakram and her dagger toward the demon, though they gain no purchase in her lizard skin.

217

The time to act is now.

I growl and shoot a fire stream at the demon. She turns around, her grin plastered to her face. *"Give it up, Sharpe, your cause is lost. Embrace oblivion, it's the last thing you will ever know!"*

I roar at Mamuna. *"Oblivion is yours, demon!"* I reach for my forearm and draw the Sword. The Guardswoman's armor closes around my dragon, my wings flapping gently as they gain their own armor.

Mamuna laughs. *"Come on, you can't be serious. You saw what happened to your father!"*

Yeah, I did. But you're not ready for this. I reach down and draw the Sabre. The Guardswoman's armor changes, becoming half light and half dark. I feel the weapon's power coursing through me, adding to the power the Sword gives the paladin. I'm also growing again; now I'm eye-to-eye with Mamuna.

She turns toward me. *"Very well, you're in such a damned hurry to die, I'll oblige you!"* She rushes me with the Blade held high, intending to slice me in half like she did Durga.

I've watched her swordsmanship as carefully as I dare to during this battle. She takes hard, lumberjack swings with her weapon, and nothing else: she expects the weapon's size to be to her advantage, and as such doesn't have any skill in dodging attacks or countering them. Her motions, to me, seem to come agonizingly slow. I'm easily able to avoid her attack, slicing at her back with both of my weapons.

Mamuna screams, turns around, rushes again. Same result. She's clearly getting too annoyed by this turn of events. She starts wildly swinging the Blade at me, and I alternate parries between the Sword and the Sabre. The parries are too strong for her to handle, as each one throws her further and further off balance.

She growls loudly. *"Why don't you die like an animal, you little hatchling bitch?!"* She sends a wild thrust out at me with the Blade. I knock it aside with both hands, then go for a jab toward Mamuna's chest with the Sabre. She catches the weapon in her hand and holds it at bay.

She's going to try to keep me from blocking the Blade this time.

The Blade whistles toward me, and I'm just barely able to catch it with the Sword and knock it away. The blow is hard enough to knock it out of her grip. She lets go of the Sabre and rushes for her weapon once again.

She gets the Blade in her grasp again, and swings it toward me. I catch it with the blades of both of my weapons. The impact causes another tremor to the area, with a thunderous sound made by the three blades making contact. We stand in this position for a while, both of us trying to gain any advantage.

Eventually, my strength starts to grow. I push Mamuna backward. A quick glance to either side of me can see where this newfound strength is coming from: we're being watched by almost everyone at the site. Supernaturals are cheering me on. Blueshirts are lowering their weapons, joining the supernaturals in watching us. Michi, looking extremely weak, has her gaze fixed on us. Fahaian, William, Gabe, all of them, all attention is on this fight.

219

It's their belief. They believe in me. They believe in the Guardsman.

My eyes narrow. If I could scream, I would do it. I push Mamuna back more and more. Her feet dig into the earth, now turning to mud as a heavy rain starts to fall. Her face shows her panic. She knows she's losing.

I thrust both arms forward, pushing Mamuna even further back, giving us some space. A quick prayer pops into my mind.

God, let this work! For everyone's sake, let this threat be ended!

I turn both the Sabre and the Sword toward the Blade, and very quickly cross my arms, crossing the two weapons, with the Blade at the center. The impact of the weapons is in just the right places ... the weak points in the Blade.

It breaks into three pieces. Lightning crashes down on the weapon, completing its destruction.

The Damnation Blade is no more.

Mamuna staggers away from me, holding the now impotent handle of the Blade. Her face shows her newfound fear ... now I have the advantage. I approach her, both of my weapons at the ready.

"Guardsman, please ... I beg you for mercy ... look, I'll take you up on your offer, we can compromise ..."

Sorry. You had your chance. It's too late now.

I cross my weapons once more. The Sword is on Mamuna's left shoulder. The Sabre is on her right. The demon lets out one last, frantic scream.

I spread my arms wide. Before Mamuna's head has a chance to hit the ground, the demon's entire body dissolves into dust. The Guardswoman drops to her knees, sheathing both of her weapons. The dragon starts shrinking back into my human body.

The rain courses down on me, washing away the filth of the battle, cleansing me of the blood on my hands. My mind is nearly empty, but for one thought.

We've won.

A cheer erupts from behind me, clearly the supernaturals celebrating our victory. My breathing is coming faster, as panic overcomes me. I scramble to my feet, unfurling my wings, the pain returning to my ribs.

"MOM! DAD!"

I flap hard, trying to get some lift in the weather, but the combination of the rain and my fatigue is keeping me on the ground. It's all I can do to run through the mud, out of the Ranch gates and toward where Mom and Dad last were.

When I reach them, my heart sinks. They're lying together, on a single dry patch of land being kept that way by Uncle Cyrus. He has a very sad expression on his face.

I'm panting, but I need to know. "Are they going to be okay?"

Uncle Cyrus looks up at me gravely. "I'm afraid these wounds are too grievous. I think they'll heal over time, but it's going to take a long, long time. These are wounds that magic can't help, but they're ones that time is only going to make worse before they're better."

I can't accept this. "You've gotta be able to do something! Give them your potions, work a healing spell, *anything! PLEASE!"*

221

Uncle Cyrus reaches one of his short arms to me, placing his hand on my shoulder. "I'm sorry, Alanna. The best I can do is stabilize them, so they won't die while the wounds heal, but that's all I can do."

I can't accept this at all. My cheeks are excessively damp between my emotions and the weather. I rush over to my parents' heads, placing my hands on their shoulders.

They open their eyes briefly, looking up at me. Dad smiles and asks me in a weak, whispery voice, "did you win?"

I sob loudly, nodding. "Mamuna's gone, Dad."

He shakily raises his hand up to my cheek, stroking it gently. I take his hand in mine. Mom looks over at me and smiles. "We're so proud of you." Her voice is equally as weak.

I lower my head down to theirs. "Please, Mom, Dad … hang in there, you guys are going to make it."

Mom sighs quietly. "I'm afraid this time … we might have bitten off too much."

I sob again. "No, don't say that …"

Dad shushes me. "Don't be sad, Alanna, not at all. You've made us both proud. You did what the Guardsman is tasked with, you defended life."

Mom reaches up and strokes my hair. "Our lives, their lives … the lives of everyone in the world … owe a debt to you and your friends."

I laugh sadly. "And to you, too, don't sell yourselves short."

"Maybe," Dad whispers. "Our time is done here, Alanna."

Another sob. "No, Dad, don't say that …"

"He speaks the truth," Mom replies. "Please know, Alanna, please know in the deepest part of your heart … that we love you, now and eternally."

Mom closes her eyes and takes her hand out of my hair. Dad does the same. My tears are free-flowing as my heart shatters. I gently place a kiss on each of my parents' foreheads, then allow myself to give in to my grief, collapsing into a wailing, tearful ball, even as the others rush over to us.

Chapter Twenty-One: A New Life

August 31st

I'm done crying. Forever.

Even through the saddest day of my life, and at the same time what should have been the most triumphant day of my life, I found that I could still be inspired. My parents' prone bodies were carried from the battlefield by a diverse group that included supernaturals, Jordanians, and blueshirts. Working together, they carried Mom and Dad into the last surviving section of the Ranch house, the area where all the bedrooms are. Under the shelter of the remnants of the roof, all of the mages … including Uncle Cyrus and Michi … cast a stasis spell over the two of them. They're now in a state of suspended animation, to allow their wounds the time to heal.

If they ever heal.

I've spent the time since the battle recovering, both physically and mentally. Every time I close my eyes, though, I see how the battle could have gone differently … I see Mamuna still in my dreams, fighting her way through the Avalon door, see her plunging the Damnation Blade into the soil. I watch in horror in my nightmares as the Lady of the Lake collapses in her death throes, as Avalon's lush landscape becomes a charred wasteland. More disturbingly, though, I watch everyone around me, every person I love and hold dear, as they writhe in agony, with a pain that I share.

I always awaken with a start from these dreams to this new reality. A reality where I have no parents anymore, but there also is no more threat to Avalon.

The only thing that's been keeping me from going completely crazy has been William's loyalty and his love. Even Michi hasn't been able to snap me out of this funk. William, bless him, has been understanding of my needs. He helps me through the nightmares, cuddles away my tears, and helps me get back to sleep.

Maybe someday they'll stop coming. For now, I'm content with the help when they *do* come.

I awaken this morning with the familiar feeling of William's arms around me. He helps me to get dressed, and out to the makeshift dining room, which is currently being rebuilt by some former blueshirts and a few of the supernaturals. Jerry Tile is among them, his ability to reconstruct non-living things coming in handy. Aunt Kitty, getting around in a wheelchair, slides a plate of breakfast to both me and William once we're at the table.

"Today's the day," she says to me, almost somberly. I nod at the reminder, starting my meal.

William puts his hand on mine, squeezing it gently. "Are you going to be all right with this?" His voice expresses his concern.

"Yeah. I have to be, I think."

"You don't have to, Alanna. This is a rough thing to do for anyone, and especially …"

I give William a sharp glance. "I'll be okay." I shove an egg in my mouth and chew a little more vigorously than I probably mean to. William shrugs, squeezes my hand again, and turns to his own plate.

Michi and Fahaian come up to the table and sit down with us. They're holding hands a lot ever since Fahaian came back. Michi looks very happy, leaning against his shoulder with her head.

"You look chipper," I comment to my best friend.

"Can you blame me?" She cuddles closer to the king. "Listen, we wanted to ask you guys something."

William smiles. "Sure, what is it?"

Fahaian clears his throat. "Will you two be free in around three weeks?"

I exchange confused looks with William, then turn back to reply. "Sure, I think so. Why?"

Michi grins wider, clutching tight to the king. "We need a best man and a maid of honor."

I reach my hand across to Michi, and I can't help but smile. "That's great! Of course we'll help out. Congratulations."

Michi beams, cuddling closer to Fahaian. He responds by actually wrapping his arm around the cat girl, as he turns to speak with us. "You both of course will be honored guests of the Kingdom of Jordan. It is going to be a good opportunity for the world to see supernaturals in a normal light, now that the Regents are gone."

That's the truth, at least. Whatever influence Mamuna held over the New Empire party appears to have completely vanished after her demise. Although we have no television, we've gotten word through more traditional media … newspapers … that all of the former loyalists to the New Empire party have rejected their affiliation and returned to their original parties.

The new President, formerly the Speaker of the House, has started moving on urging Congress and the states to rescind many of the Regents' policies.

Hellish influence can only go so far, I suppose.

Uncle Cyrus walks into the dining room, dressed in what I can only describe as a traditional wizard's robe, royal purple and hanging loosely off of his body. He motions toward us. "It's time, folks."

We all get up from the table. Aunt Kitty wheels along with us, as we all head for the Avalon door. It opens very slowly. One at a time, the entire group of us crosses into the magic realm. When we emerge, Avalon is as sunny and beautiful as it always is, and we all gather by a particular knoll, next to a familiar pond.

Two years ago, William and I were swimming here, getting to know each other better and growing our relationship. I can't believe we're back for this different purpose today.

There's some chairs set up next to the knoll. All of us take seats, except for Aunt Kitty, who pulls her wheelchair up next to Michi and Fahaian. From behind the entire group of us, Gabe walks up to the knoll, a solemn expression on his face.

"Thank you all for coming," Gabe intones. "We are here to celebrate the lives of two allies, two friends, and two dearly loved ones. Even as they slumber here, we will keep them in our hearts forever, our memories of their deeds on Earth always fresh in our minds."

Gabe motions to the other side of us. A group of eight people … three supernaturals I recognize and five blueshirts that I have never seen before … very slowly approach the knoll, carrying on their shoulders a wide wooden plank. They pass by us, moving to the knoll itself, where they remove their precious cargo and lower it into place.

Mom and Dad. They've been dressed in what appears to be medieval clothing. Dad wears what I've been told is standard attire for a knight, a long tunic over a chainmail shirt with leather pants and boots. Mom wears a long, flowing gown of white, which contrasts greatly with her green, scaled flesh.

Two things strike me even more emotionally than just simply their presence. One is the Sabre, which is held in Dad's left hand, like it's at the ready for him to draw and become the Penitent at any time.

The other is that they're holding hands.

I said I was done crying, but I lied, because fresh tears are coming as I look upon my prone parents and gently run my fingers around the Sharpe watch, hanging from my left wrist. William pats my arm as he senses me getting emotional. Gabe nods his thanks to the honor guard as he continues his speech.

"Cole Sharpe was the Guardsman, a true friend and hero. He stood up to the evils that threatened all life, everywhere, and never flinched. He stood with the forces of life, as a reliable ally. Most of all, he was a loving man. He loved his wife dearly. He loved his daughter just as much.

"Ariel Vibria was also briefly a Guardsman, loyal and honest to the end. She had her powers thrust upon her, without her permission, but she did what she could. Although sometimes darkness threatened to claim her, she rose above it. She found love in Cole, a love that did literally save a life by transcending death itself. That love produced a beautiful daughter, and inspired many.

"Together, Cole and Ariel defended life as best as they could. They fell as heroes, never as cowards. We will … always remember them this way."

If I'm not mistaken, Gabe was starting to choke up near the end there. *If there's one thing that man is incapable of being, it's emotional. This must have really hurt him.*

Gabe turns and nods toward the pond. The water rushes toward the center, from which rises the Lady of the Lake, her watery face showing her sadness at this occasion equals ours. She reaches out from the pond toward the knoll, a dome of water emerging from her hand and completely surrounding Mom and Dad.

"These honored heroes shall slumber here, until their nation calls upon them once more. Cole Sharpe and Ariel Vibria, the Penitent and the dragon, they shall be remembered and loved by those who they served in life."

The dome now completely encloses around the bodies of Mom and Dad, as the Lady lifts the new globe of water up from the knoll. She pulls the sphere close to her chest, sinking back down into the pond with it. In a matter of seconds, they're all gone.

Farewell, Mom and Dad. I love you.

More tears fall. I'm only stopped from falling into full-throated crying by a shadow passing over us. I look up and spot a winged man, who's sprinkling white flower petals down on us, a tribute to my parents. I can't help now but to smile as I recognize Carlos del Aire, offering his condolences.

When he passes by the sun, my eyes remain fixed on the orb. I almost can see two figures, one male and one female, silhouetted in the rays. They grasp each other's hands, and appear to look back toward me. Wings sprout from the female silhouette, as the male one waves. The female figure collects the male one in her arms, flaps her wings, and ascends into the light.

They're together forever.

"Alanna?" William's voice breaks my reverie. "How do you feel?"

I turn my face away from the sunlight, back to the face of my own beloved. His cheeks are glistening, too. I reach up and stroke one of his cheeks before I answer him.

"I feel … loved. Loved and alive, and so happy to be both." We wrap our arms around each other, standing up and heading back for the door, back to the Ranch and the real world.

September 27th

The room is ornately decorated, with a large vanity and mirror on one wall. The rest of the room is filled with dress forms, makeup kits, and other things. I've just shooed a lot of the attendants out of the place, because things are going to get wild enough without them in the room. All that's left in here is me and Uncle Cyrus.

"Is it safe?" Michi's voice squeaks.

"Yeah, they're gone. Come on out," I answer.

The door to the adjoining room, a bathroom, clicks open, and out emerges a sight that I never thought I would see. Michika Salem, my best friend … my sister in heart if not in blood … emerges in one of the most ornate bridal gowns I've ever seen. It's cut low on her chest, giving her slight cleavage, and shoulderless. The bustle of the gown drops all the way to the floor, including a nine-foot train. On her head, pinned to the alternating black-and-orange hair, sits a delicate tiara, 55 diamonds creating even more sparkle to the outfit. The gown and crown stand in stark contrast to the woman wearing them, her cat's fur in orange, black, and yellow creating a definite dividing line where the top of the dress lies, not to mention the gauntlet covering her entire left arm.

She looks very embarrassed as she looks up at us. "I look stupid, don't I?"

Uncle Cyrus stands slack-jawed. I giggle slightly. "Not at all, Michi. You're beautiful, and Fahaian's going to love it."

She seems to take a sigh of relief. "Oh thank God, I'm glad for that." She comes over to us. "Thanks for helping me, guys." She hugs both me and Uncle Cyrus.

231

"Thank you for letting us come," I respond. Playfully, when she releases the hug, I curtsy to her. "Your Highness."

Michi giggles. "Oh come on, Alanna." She hugs me tighter. "Sisters, to the end, remember?"

I smile warmly, returning the hug. "To the end. Always."

The first vestiges of music start playing. I rush out of the dressing room to take my place next to William, looking sharp himself in his best suit.

"How is she?" he asks.

"Nervous as hell, classic Michi though." I loop my arm through William's, just as we're given our cue to walk down the aisle.

It seems odd, how Western this ceremony is. Fahaian insisted on it, although he has some vestiges of his Zoroastrian traditions, such as two priests at the head of the aisle, a fire censer standing behind them rather than an altar, and two chairs where the couple will sit. We'll be standing the whole time, so I hope the new shoes I'm wearing break in really soon.

Once we've made our way to either side of the chairs, Uncle Cyrus and Michi enter, as the music increases in volume. They take a long time to reach the end of the aisle, but when they do Michi gently kisses her dad on the forehead before taking her place in the chair next to me.

All attention returns to the head of the aisle as Fahaian enters, in an entirely white outfit from head to toe, with the exception of a square black hat. We were told this was also going to follow the traditions; Aunt Kitty is there to greet him, holding herself up with a pair of metal braces around her still-recovering legs.

She puts her thumb to Fahaian's forehead, leaving a traditional mark on it. He bows to thank her, then continues up the aisle, taking his place in the last empty chair.

One of the priests begins the ceremony, asking for the couple's consent. A ribbon is tied around their right hands, joining them, while they are entirely wrapped with another long ribbon. A long, muttering prayer is being spoken all the while by the other priest, one that I can't quite understand, but sounds very solemn. Fahaian and Michi reach down next to themselves with their free hands, into a basket holding rice, and throw the rice over each other.

This raises applause from the assembly. The first priest raises his hands over the couple. "May the Creator, the omniscient Lord, grant you a progeny of sons and grandsons, plenty of means to provide for yourselves, heart-ravishing friendship, bodily strength, long life, and an existence of one hundred and fifty years!"

That's a bit of an odd benediction, but it's not my place to judge.

The ceremony quickly turns back to Western at this point, as Fahaian and Michi are given permission to kiss each other. This kiss lasts a long, almost uncomfortable time. When they finally disengage, they've been untied from the chairs, and are able to stand up. The second priest steps in front of them and kneels.

"I am honored to be before you. All present, please kneel in the presence of His Royal Highness King Fahaian and Her Royal Highness Queen Michika!"

The entire assembly rises, then falls to their knees. Fahaian motions toward the fire censer behind the priests, and apparently uses his telepyretic abilities because the next sound I hear is gasping and flapping. I look up and see that he's produced doves of fire, which now fly overhead.

We all cheer. It's kind of sad for me, because I know this means Michi stays here, but at the same time I'm happy for her. I sincerely hope she and Fahaian reign for a long time, and I know that this won't be the last time I see my best friend.

October 29th

Why am I nervous? I've done so much more than this.

I'm pacing back and forth in my room at the Ranch, fully rebuilt now since the battle. I've been waiting all day for this, and now I'm starting to get really nervous. I need someone to calm me down.

On cue almost, Aunt Kitty walks in. "Are you ready?"

"As ready as I get," I respond. She's loaned me some more clothes, including the white dress I'm currently wearing, which hugs every curve and contour of my body. Am I nervous because this shows me off so much?

"Good, 'cause everyone's waiting outside." She rocks her head back. "Come on."

She walks out of the room. I take a deep breath, closing my eyes to gather my nerves. Finally, when they're as gathered as they're ever going to be, I open the door and step out into the hallway.

The rebuilding of the Ranch got done shortly after we came back from Jordan. Michi and Fahaian have been keeping close tabs on our progress, and are promising to visit next month for Thanksgiving. In the meantime, things have gotten better, both here and around the country. The new President's initiatives to overturn the Regents' policies passed unanimously, and we're expecting that by this time next year we'll once more be living in the United States of America rather than the New Empire. Supernaturals have regained their civil rights, and started working alongside regular humans to create a better world. Sure, there's still some problems from time to time, but nothing that it's necessary to create a totalitarian regime over.

I begin walking up the hallway. The local changes pop into mind. A few of the supernaturals, myself included, have been taken in at the Ranch and made this place a home. We work for Aunt Kitty and Uncle Cyrus, tending to their herds of bison and keeping ourselves productive around the place. The Avalon door remains behind the house, and we've been slowly starting to repatriate all the supernaturals we ferried through it. Old wounds have been mended, especially ones that we thought never would heal; for instance, Durga's been allowed to come visit again, and now she spends time with Aunt Kitty passing old war stories back and forth. I always look forward to the goddess's visits, and although her recovery from her Damnation Blade wound has been slow, it's progressing.

I'm nearly at the end of the hallway. It's stunning to me how much change has taken place ... and there's one more change that's about to come. On the opposite end of the house, the party's all there, waiting for me.

Many familiar faces line the room, this place where we planned strategies and recovered from battles. Teresa Gracin, cradling her shortened arm close to her, still weeps for her lost husband; the sadness in her is tempered only slightly by the gentle tummy bump she displays, the final gift Trent left her. Julian and Grandmother stand close to the other end of the room, holding hands and smiling back at me. Jerry Tile, the very first supernatural we rescued from the SSA, pats my shoulder as I pass him by. Gabe stands at the hearth, his little book in hand. Aunt Kitty and Uncle Cyrus are on either side of him.

Next to Uncle Cyrus, dressed to the nines and looking just as nervous as I feel, is William.

I can't blame us for being nervous. How often do you get your own wedding day, anyway?

I walk all the way up the aisle, taking my place at William's side. My attention kind of focuses on Gabe, whose eyes look to us for attention.

"Dearly beloved, human and supernatural alike, we are gathered here in this new era of peace and citizenship to join these two souls … these two strong wills … Alanna Sharpe and William White Bear … in the holiest of covenants, the bonds of marriage."

The ceremony is a blur, as my mind is so focused on the changes that have taken place. I'm vaguely aware when we're asked to exchange rings, and the re-application of the Petoskey stone ring to my finger brings my attention back to the present. Then I look at William, and I remember why this was all worth it. *The people I love are safe, sound, and never have to fear genocide.*

Gabe smiles the warmest I've ever seen him smile as he intones his words. "Do you, William White Bear, take this woman, Alanna Ariel Sharpe, as your lawfully wedded wife, to have and to hold, for richer or poorer, in sickness and health, 'til death do you part?"

William smiles wider. "Beyond death, I do."

Gabe nods serenely. "And do you, Alanna Ariel Sharpe, take this man, William White Bear, as your lawfully wedded husband, to have and to hold, for richer or poorer, in sickeness and health, 'til death do you part?"

I smile at Gabe, and at William. "Forever and always, I do."

Gabe nods. "Then there's not much left for me to do. By the power vested in me by my Employer, by the State of Wyoming, and by what will soon be once again the United States of America, I now pronounce you husband and wife." He reaches out and hugs us, just like he hugged Teresa and Trent.

When he does, he whispers in my ear. "You will always be the ultimate Guardsman in my eyes, Alanna. Congratulations."

I smile wider and nearly weep at those words, as he turns us around. "Ladies and gentlemen, allow me to present Mr. and Mrs. William and Alanna White Bear. You may now kiss the bride."

We've been waiting for this all day. William takes my chin in his hand, lowers his face down to me, and kisses me with all the love and devotion he can muster. On my hip, I can feel the Sword warming up.

Mom and Dad are happy.

I return the kiss as eagerly. It's a grand way to begin a new life, for ourselves and everyone around the world.

Transcriber's Epilogue

I was in tears by the time I finished the last of the journals. In my time in hiding, I'd tried to avoid any news coming from the New Empire, so seeing from one of my best friends in the supernatural community that it was going away was a great and welcome surprise. That and the two marriages in the end, these were making me emotional. Maybe my wife and daughter would be released soon!

I removed the special reading glasses, and time resumed its normal passage. The books returned to a scribble of runic gibberish, unintelligible to any except the people they were intended to be read by. I took a deep breath, and it felt extremely good. I guess I had been holding my breath since I had read Alanna's battle with Mamuna, and simply forgotten about it, caught up in the story as I was.

I returned the last journal to the box, accidentally knocking over the newspaper, the one I'd propped up which announced a prisoner amnesty. When I did, I spotted the last of the contents of the package, a small, folded-over note. I reached into the box and withdrew the card. Thankfully, I didn't have to put the glasses back on to read it, but what surprised me about it was that it only had one line, written in a feminine hand.

LOOK OUTSIDE YOUR WINDOW! -AWB

I puzzled over this message for a while, particularly who did I know that had the initials AWB? My eyes widened when the realization hit me: AWB was Alanna. Alanna White Bear. I threw the note aside and ran to my window, opening it with shaking hands and sticking my head outside.

On the sidewalk, three stories down, stood a very happy party, smiling up at me. A tall blond woman, cuddling arm-in-arm with her escort, an even taller heavily muscled man, stood behind the two people I had been waiting to see for years.

My wife and daughter.

I bolted out of my apartment, down the stairs, and out the door, clutching my family tightly to me once again. This close to the party, I finally realized that the blond woman was Alanna, which would make her escort the man she had married, William White Bear. These thoughts were buried by my happiness at being reunited with my family.

That was four years ago.

As I write these words this evening, I'm awaiting my cue to take the stage at a victory rally in Wyoming, at the Hidden-In-Plain-Sight Ranch. I can hear the crowd outside, clamoring for the guest of honor, who I'm supposed to introduce.

Change came quickly once the New Empire regime was taken down. Presidential elections were just re-established this year, after allowing the former House Speaker to serve out a full term. Over the course of two years, a constitutional amendment overturning the Regents' power grab was unanimously ratified by the remaining states, and olive branches were extended to the independent republics of Alaska and Texas to coax them to rejoin the Union. A concerted effort was made by the re-established in their power Congress to affect changes across the board to all social and military programs. The SSA was disbanded, returned to its original military and law enforcement purposes. An additional division was made out of the former blueshirts, which was tasked with beginning cleanup and recovery duties in the Missouri Rad Zone, with the goal of making the state habitable for human/supernatural residents once more.

Which leads us to tonight. This year has been the most good-natured Presidential election cycle in recent memory, since it's been so long since there's actually been an election. It culminates in this celebration tonight.

A knock comes on my door. When I answer it, standing there is Alanna White Bear, holding her one-year-old son Julian. "It's time."

I smile back at my friend, whose journals I had the privilege of transcribing. "How's married life treating you?"

"Pretty well. I'm about to finish college this year, so is William, and everyone at the Ranch has been so helpful with the baby."

"I can imagine, he's quite the cutie." I pinch the tot's cheek. He grins and giggles, shrinking back toward his mommy, but still showing signs of his supernatural nature, a pair of vestigial wings that I've been told on several occasions, by both Alanna and William, will never work. "I remember you when you were not much older than Julian here, you did many of the same things as I recall."

She nods, wistfully. "Those were the days, huh?"

"They were." I clear my throat, collecting my notes. "Okay, I'm ready."

Alanna leads me out the door, to a stage set up just outside the foyer of the Ranch house. It's coated entirely in crepe paper and patriotic bunting. I spot my wife and daughter, sitting to one side with William White Bear, and they wave to me. I wave back, then make my way on the stage, adjusting the microphone slightly so that it comes to my mouth.

"Ladies and gentlemen, thank you for coming here tonight. We're here for a most auspicious occasion. Let me tell you, I've known the people you've come to see for a while, through their actions and their friends. I can think of no one else better suited for this honor which is about to be bestowed. So without further ado, please allow me to introduce to you a combat veteran, a dedicated parent, an honorable individual who showed the nation what their true colors were. Ladies and gentlemen, I present to you the President-Elect of the United States, Kitty Salem!"

I turn and applaud, and from behind me approaches the entire extended Salem family. Kitty is the first to walk out, waving enthusiastically to the crowd, limping slightly from the injury she incurred at the final battle. Cyrus accompanies her, not bothering with a HoSIP to make himself look taller; he's apparently embraced his shortness finally, after so long. Behind them enter royalty, King Fahaian and Queen Michika, looking just as overjoyed as Michika's parents, leading their toddler daughter Princess Akiko for a while before the queen finally picks her up.

Kitty comes over to the podium and embraces me. "Layin' it on a little thick, aren't you?" she whispers.

"You deserve the praise," I respond. "Now get out there and talk to your people!"

I release the embrace and cross the stage, back to where my own family sits in waiting. My wife turns and whispers to me. "Did you ever think that one interview so long ago would lead to this?"

I smile back at her, as confetti starts to fall. "It was a really wild ride."

She takes my right hand, as my daughter takes my left, and we watch Kitty give her victory speech. Hope rises in my soul, hope for humanity and for the world. If a nation that so shunned supernaturals just barely five years ago can embrace one as their President, there's truly hope for us as beings of mercy and love. Alanna's story shows what power love and loyalty hold, even in today's modern society.

– Don A. Martinez
November 4th, 2036

Acknowledgments

Congratulations. If you are reading these words, it means you have reached the conclusion of the *Phantom Squadron* cycle, and the culmination of a story that has kept my mind captive for more than a decade. Above and beyond that first volume in 2009, this series has been buoyed by numerous people over the years.

In its initial incarnation as a screenplay, *Phantom Squadron*'s first audience came from the users of the now-defunct Hollywood simulation Film-Mogul, whose feedback on the work helped to cement, in my mind, the fact that there truly *was* an audience for my brand of intellectual pulp fiction. To those earliest readers who followed CIBO #A13 even before they were designated as such, I thank you for your encouragement.

The Advance Guard was written as a class project for a Craft of Writing course at Buffalo State College. For encouraging me to the point that I put it out for mass audiences, I have to thank Dr. Ralph Wahlstrom, esteemed writing professor and author of one of the best writer's advice books I've ever read, *The Tao of Writing.*

My sincerest thanks go out to those intrepid souls who run the Office of Letters and Light in San Francisco, better known as the international organizers of National Novel Writing Month every year; three of the books in *Phantom Squadron* were NaNo entrants, with two winners *(Dinétah Dragon* and *Eden Inviolate* were both written in their entireties during November 2010 and 2012, respectively).

In spirit, I would like to pay respect to Dante Alighieri, whose visionary work *The Divine Comedy* served as the inspiration and backbone of *Infernal Eighteen.*

My deepest regards go to all of the friends I have made both through the East Texas Writers Association and in my time as the publisher of Desert Coyote Productions; in particular, thanks go out to my fellow DCP authors who have given support of my efforts: Patty Wiseman, Jeannie Faulkner Barber, Lynn Hobbs, Denny Youngblood, Teresa Richenberger, and Bernadette Thompson Martin.

Last and most certainly not least, I give my greatest thanks and appreciation to the women in my life who have served as inspiration, muses, and sources for my work. To my mother Joanne Hicks, who allowed me to cultivate writing as a talent. To my daughter Kahlan Martinez, born in the middle of writing *Infernal Eighteen,* for granting my life more focus above and beyond writing. And finally, to my beloved wife Stacey Martinez, who to this day still serves as my muse and inspiration for living day to day. You are all Alanna; you are all Ariel; you are all Michika; you are all Kitty in my heart, and I have naught but eternal love for you all.